## "Cord, Please Don't Force Something Between Us."

Abbie saw his jaw clench even tighter. "Don't ruin—"

"Ruin what, Abbie? We walk on eggshells around each other. We never talk about anything really important, like that night, for instance." He saw the color rising in her face.

"And don't be embarrassed, dammit! Why shouldn't we talk about it? We made a baby that night. How can you pretend it never happened? You wrote me off, Abbie, when you found out about the baby. You never once considered coming to me in an honest, open way and discussing the situation. I want to know why you thought pussyfooting around the truth was your only recourse."

Abbie drew a shaky breath. It was time for the bald-faced truth. Her lips parted to speak, to tell him that he had been such a complete stranger to her when she discovered her condition, her only recourse *had* been deception.

But speaking at all was suddenly impossible, because Cord was kissing her.

Dear Reader,

This month we have a very special treat in store for you. It's the Silhouette Desire "Premiere" author for 1993! This is a completely new, never-before-published writer, who we have chosen as someone exciting and outstanding. Her name is Carol Devine, and her book is *Beauty and the Beastmaster*. There is a letter in it from her to all of you, her new fans. *Who* is the Beauty and just who—or what—is the Beastmaster? Well, I'm not telling; you'll have to read and find out.

In addition to our "Premiere" author, October has five more favorites. Our *Man of the Month* is from the delightful Cait London. The lineup is completed with wonderful books by Jackie Merritt, Christine Rimmer, Noelle Berry McCue and Shawna Delacorte.

As for *next* month . . . it's a winner! We've decided to "Heat Up Your Winter" with six of our most sensuous, most spectacular authors: Ann Major, Dixie Browning, Barbara Boswell, Robin Elliott, Mary Lynn Baxter and Lass Small. Silhouette Desire . . . you just can't get *any* better than this.

All the best,

Lucia Macro
Senior Editor

# JACKIE MERRITT
## IMITATION LOVE

SILHOUETTE *Desire*

Published by Silhouette Books New York

America's Publisher of Contemporary Romance

**SILHOUETTE BOOKS**
300 East 42nd St., New York, N.Y. 10017

IMITATION LOVE

Copyright © 1993 by Carolyn Joyner

All rights reserved. Except for use in any review, the reproduction or utilization of this work in whole or in part in any form by any electronic, mechanical or other means, now known or hereafter invented, including xerography, photocopying and recording, or in any information storage or retrieval system, is forbidden without the permission of the publisher, Silhouette Books, 300 E. 42nd St., New York, N.Y. 10017

ISBN: 0-373-05813-6

First Silhouette Books printing October 1993

All the characters in this book have no existence outside the imagination of the author and have no relation whatsoever to anyone bearing the same name or names. They are not even distantly inspired by any individual known or unknown to the author, and all incidents are pure invention.

® and ™:Trademarks used with authorization. Trademarks indicated with ® are registered in the United States Patent and Trademark Office, the Canada Trade Mark Office and in other countries.

**Printed in the U.S.A.**

**Books by Jackie Merritt**

Silhouette Desire

## *JACKIE MERRITT*

and her husband live just outside of Las Vegas, Nevada. An accountant for many years, Jackie has happily traded numbers for words. Next to family, books are her greatest joy. She started writing in 1987 and her efforts paid off in 1988 with the publication of her first novel. When she's not writing or enjoying a good book, Jackie dabbles in watercolor painting and has been known to tickle the ivories in her spare time.

# One

────

**S**omehow Abbie Forbes made it from the Women's Clinic to her car, but once behind the wheel she sat and stared, her body stiff, her gray green eyes disbelieving. Anyone walking past would have simply seen an attractive thirtyish woman with glossy, honey-blond hair and a pretty face looking into space, perhaps daydreaming.

Abbie wasn't dreaming, although the last hour definitely bore a nightmarish quality. *Pregnant!* The word itself felt like something alien. She couldn't ask herself how—she knew how. But it didn't seem possible that one misstep, which she only barely remembered, could have such an enormous consequence.

"My Lord," she whispered in a wave of confused anguish. Dr. Leighton had been adamant: she was pregnant. The baby would be born in September.

Unless she had an abortion. She was only six weeks along and abortion was a feasible option.

A shudder shook Abbie's small-boned frame. The abortion issue had always been far distanced from her own reality. Debating the pros and cons of the question in regard to other people was infinitely different than applying them to herself.

Abortion was out. That was the only thing she knew with any degree of certainty.

Finding that mobility was returning to her numb limbs, Abbie started the car and put it in gear. She slowly maneuvered through the busy parking lot and entered traffic. She was due back at the station, having taken a long lunch hour to see Dr. Leighton, but the car headed in the opposite direction, as if by its own will.

Mistake, error, blunder. The synonymous words stacked up in Abbie's mind while she drove. The worst part to face was that she hardly remembered that night in December.

Abbie brushed away a tear, angry that self-pity dared to intrude at a time like this. It wasn't pity she needed, it was some answers, such as what she was going to do now. She hadn't been married for sixteen months, not since Nick died. As far as friends and co-workers knew, she hadn't even dated.

Tears threatened again. That December night hadn't been a date, dammit, it had been a one-night stand! Things like this didn't happen to women like her. She had a job, a career and hordes of respect. Her face was known all over southern Nevada, visible every week night as she co-anchored the six o'clock news with Ron Harrison.

Abbie's heart leaped into her throat at the thought of Ron. Handsome, charming Ron, who would just as soon destroy her face-to-face as stab her in the back. Off camera, Ron barely spoke to her. This would be precisely the ammunition he'd been praying for to get her out of that co-anchor chair and give him the number one position with the television station, a position she'd worked long and hard to attain.

She couldn't be fired for extramarital pregnancy, but she could be asked to step out of the spotlight. Of course she had a contract and could hire a lawyer. But the station had more money and could hire a bus of lawyers and in the end, Abbie knew, if they wanted her out, she'd be out. Feeling weak suddenly, Abbie pulled over to the side of the road and stopped the car. She'd driven south and was in a less populated sector of the immense Vegas valley. Her fingertips left the steering wheel and rose to her temples, where tension was building. The past Christmas season flicked through her mind.

She had deliberately avoided thinking about that night since its advent, and now, dredging up details wasn't that easy to do. Some of it was clear, the earlier portion of the evening. She'd been working like a Trojan on projects that always gained momentum during the Christmas season, gifts for foster children and food and shelter for the homeless in particular. Rushing from one thing to another never, ever annoyed her, but it was tiring. There were at least a dozen Christmas parties requiring an appearance, which she sandwiched in between more important activities. Everyone at the station was doing the same. KSTV's manager, Bob Sidwell, insisted on his staff's involvement in civic affairs, which kept the independent station in the foreground of the broadcasting community and before the public.

Abbie loved her job and was positive that being too busy to think about herself was what had brought her through Nick's long illness and death. She hadn't survived the heartbreaking ordeal unscathed, no one would. But there were moments when she was proud of surviving it at all. She'd done some serious changing, of course. It had taken time to laugh spontaneously again, and she had absolutely no urges toward the opposite sex. Which made that one night so mystifying.

Her co-workers had dragged her along to another party, one that she had hoped to avoid. It wasn't on her mental list of necessary duties and for days she'd been working practically nonstop. Not only that, she'd had a dental appointment that afternoon, which had left her feeling slightly woozy. A deep inner exhaustion demanded that she go home and crawl into bed, but her cheerful companions ignored her protests, and she found herself being hauled across town, riding in Julie Elkins's car with two other women, all of them chattering a mile a minute and laughing at every little thing.

By the time they reached their destination, a large, gorgeous home, Abbie was relaxing and joining in the merriment. The party's hosts were a well-known couple, although Abbie hadn't personally met them before. Their house was fabulous and decorated to the nines with Christmas ornaments. People were everywhere, many of them known to Abbie and to whom she said a cheery hello. A glass of champagne was pressed into her hand. She lost track of Julie and the other women she'd come with, but she barely noticed. It was, Abbie realized, the first party she had enjoyed in a long, long time.

Later, the next morning especially, she realized something else: that first glass of champagne had hit her hard, and she had no idea of how many had followed.

In retrospect the rest of the evening was a blur. She knew there was a man. She remembered his name, Cord Durant, and that he was big and incredibly good-looking. She recalled that he'd made her laugh, repeatedly, and that they'd danced together. The music had been provided by a live band and was marvelous. There'd been a huge buffet table loaded with delicious food, and the champagne had never stopped flowing.

Sitting in her car with the motor idling, Abbie massaged her aching temples. Her next lucid memory of the whole fiasco was of the next morning. She'd awakened in a strange bed with a strange man, Cord Durant, without a stitch of clothing on her body. There was no whitewashing the awful truth: she'd made love with a man she didn't know.

She had lain there, frozen with shock, barely noticing the ghastly aching of her head. Then, finally, she'd silently gotten out of that king-size bed and found her clothing strewn throughout the bedroom and living room. She was dressed and starting out of the large apartment when she heard, "Please don't leave like this."

She whirled and nearly blacked out from the dizziness in her throbbing head. "I . . . tried not to wake you."

"Obviously."

The man had pulled on a pair of gray sweatpants and nothing else. Abbie took one look and averted her eyes. All the while her brain kept refusing to believe, fervently denying what had taken place here with this total stranger. "I have to go home and get ready for work."

"It's early. We could have breakfast together first."

"No... no, I..."

He crossed the room to stand before her. "Abbie, look at me."

She didn't. She couldn't.

Her feet nervously carried her to the door. She stopped to say one thing. "I'm sorry this happened. Goodbye, Mr. Durant."

"After last night, you're calling me mister?"

"Uh... sorry." If only she could remember! She was embarrassed nearly to tears, so regretful she wished she could die on the spot.

He strode to a table bearing a telephone, scribbled something on a piece of paper and brought it to her. "Take this. It's my telephone number. I'd like you to call when you're feeling better."

"I feel fine," she said stiffly, but took the paper and dropped it in her purse. She still couldn't look at him.

"May I have your number?"

"Um... I'd rather not. Goodbye." She dashed from the apartment, aware that he'd followed her to the door and was standing there watching her. In the corridor, which went in two directions, she stopped, confused, to wonder which way to go.

"The elevator's to the left," Cord Durant said quietly.

"Thank you." Without looking back she hurried down the corridor, located the elevator and only breathed when she was within the small compartment and speeding down to the first floor.

She noticed one thing upon exiting the building, its bright red front doors. After that she hailed a passing taxi.

She hadn't called Cord Durant.

She had pushed the whole terrible incident into the farthest reaches of her mind, vowing to forget it. Everyone made at least one ghastly mistake in his life: Cord Durant was hers.

Who could ever have imagined such a result as the one she had been hit with from one mistake?

Who was Cord Durant? What kind of man was he? She hadn't asked anyone, she hadn't even mentioned his name to a soul. Who knew him? There was possibly a connection between him and the party's hosts, but that wasn't a given as she herself hadn't known the couple and had still attended their party. The invitation, Abbie recalled, had been issued to the TV station, not to individuals.

And then, out of the blue, sitting in her car with the motor idling, something happened that startled Abbie. For the first time since Dr. Leighton's edict, she thought of her condition in terms of the child. *A baby!* A rocketing joy shot through Abbie, a sensation that was completely out of her control and beyond reason.

How she had wanted a baby during her and Nick's sad marriage. His illness had been discovered within months of their wedding. They had talked about children but were both glad they hadn't hastily started a family. All of their strength and effort had gone into battling Nick's illness, and neither had mentioned children again.

And now, because of exhaustion, a stint in her dentist's chair and too much champagne, a child was going to become a reality. Decisions must be made, about her job, about the child, about her life.

But not right this minute. Taking a deep breath, Abbie put the car in gear and stepped on the gas. Regardless of circumstances, she had dawdled as long as she dared. She was due back at the station.

Going into his condominium, Cord switched on the living-room TV set and continued on to the kitchen to get a beer from the refrigerator. He brought a cold bottle back to the living room and settled down on the sofa, kicking off his shoes and propping his feet on the coffee table.

"Good evening. I'm Ron Harrison."

"I'm Abbie Forbes, and this is the six o'clock news. Today in Las Vegas, Metro police have been investigating..."

Cord barely listened. Through squinted eyes he watched very closely, however. Abbie Forbes, mystery lady. Sexy as sin and cold as ice. Was she a split personality? He'd known she'd been tipsy that night, but tipsy wasn't drunk in his book. The next morning she'd run as though the devil himself had been on her heels.

The TV screen flashed on a crime scene, then back to Abbie. She's pretty, Cord thought, as he did every time he caught her news broadcast. She had a great voice and an incredible smile. He liked looking at her, always had. Meeting her at that party had been exciting, and then when she'd been so warm and responsive, dancing with him, enjoying the same silly jokes, he'd felt something important developing.

Yes, it had surprised him that she'd so readily agreed to deserting the party and coming to his place. But she'd giggled about sneaking off, treating the whole thing as some sort of prank.

He'd kissed her, what man wouldn't have? A beautiful, sensual woman? Any man would have kissed her. What he hadn't expected was so much passion from her.

He also hadn't expected what happened the next morning, waking up to hear her tiptoeing from the apartment.

She hadn't called him and he had hoped she would. It would be a simple matter for him to contact her. All he'd have to do was drive up to the TV station and walk into the place. But every time he had just about decided to do it, he remembered how embarrassed she had seemed that morning.

Embarrassed. That word bothered Cord. Remembering the entire episode bothered Cord. Maybe she had another man. That would be one explanation for her behaviour. He'd never know if it was the right one. Yet, he was drawn to watch Abbie's broadcast at every opportunity. He was in and out of town as he maintained a photographic studio in Los Angeles as well as the one in Vegas, which required a great deal of flying back and forth. But he did all his own photography, specializing in portraits, and through the years had built an impressive reputation in the field. His talent was indisputable. He captured moods, spirits, whatever the client wished to portray, glamour, comedy, sobriety, playfulness.

He was thirty-three years old and had never been married. His friends called him a terminal bachelor, which amused him, although there was a lot of truth in the label. He had no desire to change his single status and was content with his life-style.

But Abbie bothered him, and that damned word—*embarrassed*—picked at his interior with the tenacity of a bulldog. It was probably the reason he hadn't just shown up at the TV station: he didn't want to embarrass her further.

Cord knew a few facts about Abbie Forbes, only because they were common knowledge. She was a widow and doing very well in local broadcasting. That was about it, just enough knowledge to tantalize his imagination and not enough to satisfy any of his curiosity.

The show had switched to several minutes of on-the-scene shots, then to Ron. Cord got up and went back to the refrigerator to see if there was anything in it fit to eat for dinner. When Abbie's voice became dominant again, he grabbed a stalk of celery and returned to the sofa.

This time he frowned. There was something subtly different about her this evening. What was it? Something in her eyes. Only someone with his innate sensitivity to moods would detect it, he was sure, but there was an unusual tension in her eyes. Maybe her smile wasn't as bright as it normally was. Her blouse was a great shade of gray and looked like silk, a tasteful garment as all of her on-camera clothing was. Her hair was short, about jaw-length, and styled with soft bangs brushed to the left side of her forehead.

She turned her head to say something to Ron and Cord again detected tension in her expression. His frown deepened.

The camera caught her full-face again as she turned the program over to the weatherman. Cord sat back and chewed on the celery. Ms. Forbes was as bothered by something as he was, but it was too egocentric to imagine that her tension had anything to do with him. After all, she only had to pick up the phone to reach him.

She hadn't called because she never wanted to see him again. It was a kick in the ego, but there it was, like it or not.

Suddenly disgruntled, Cord picked up the remote control and switched off the set. Watching Abbie Forbes was childish and self-punishing. Maybe he'd had enough of that.

Getting to his feet, he ambled to the kitchen to scare up some dinner.

After a week of profound soul-searching, Abbie came to one discomfiting conclusion: she had to know something about the father of her baby. It was only logical and sensible. Bearing a child without knowing something of his father's medical history was a foolish risk these days, and whatever else she did in regard to her condition, she wasn't willing to gamble with her baby's health.

She'd told no one about her pregnancy, not even her best friend, Sherry Newman. Sherry was Abbie's next-door neighbor and a working woman herself, although Sherry's field was banking. Sherry lived alone, too, as she was divorced, and the two women had become very good friends after Nick's death.

Sherry would be the first to know, Abbie never doubted, but Abbie wasn't ready to confide in anyone. First things first, she told herself, with the most crucial item on a list that threatened to become painful before completion being a meeting with Cord Durant.

But how? Certainly she didn't want to give him any foolish ideas about the two of them. The last thing she wanted was a repeat of something she couldn't even remember.

And then she did recall a bit of trivia, something about him being a portrait photographer. Had he told her about it, or had she heard it from someone else?

It didn't matter. It just possibly could be the excuse she needed for calling him.

It wasn't difficult to locate him professionally, although she had thrown away that piece of paper with his home telephone number, which she wouldn't have used in this instance anyway.

Still, it took an enormous amount of courage to dial the Durant Studio. The phone rang three times and was finally answered by a youthful male voice, certainly not the one in her memory. "Durant Studio."

Abbie cleared her throat. "Hello. I need a portrait done. Is Mr. Durant in?"

"He's in Los Angeles for a few days, but I could set you up an appointment. How does Thursday afternoon of next week sound?"

*Next week? Is he that busy?* "My weekday afternoons are swamped. Does Mr. Durant ever take clients on a Saturday?"

"Sometimes. I could check with him about it and call you back."

"Yes, that would probably be all right. Mention to him, if you will, that I need the portrait as soon as possible. My name is Abbie Forbes."

"Abbie Forbes. I'm writing it down, Ms. Forbes. Say, are you the Abbie Forbes on the six o'clock news?"

"The same."

"I watch you all the time."

Abbie smiled. "Always glad to talk to a viewer."

"I'll be talking to Cord—Mr. Durant—later today, Ms. Forbes. What's your number, so I can let you know what he says?"

Abbie recited a number. "That's the TV station. If I'm unavailable, please leave a message."

"Will do. Thanks for calling."

Putting the phone down, Abbie dried her damp palms on the legs of her slacks. All she wanted to do was meet Cord Durant again and talk to him a little. She didn't know if he was a pleasant man or a grouch, and she certainly had no idea of how he would look upon a professional appointment with her.

But there were a few questions she would like him to answer, presented subtly, of course.

When Abbie came out of a meeting with Bob Sidwell that afternoon, she was handed several telephone messages. One of them was from Danny Atkins, the young man, she assumed, who'd taken her call at the Durant Studio. The message was that Mr. Durant would meet her at his studio at ten on Saturday morning.

Abbie went to her office, closed the door and sat at her desk, suddenly shaking like a leaf. She didn't want to see

Cord Durant again, she *never* wanted to see the man again in her entire life. She didn't feel self-pity now, she felt self-disgust. How could she have done such a thing as to go to bed with a total stranger? What in God's name had possessed her that night?

And how could she be so logical one minute and so completely opposed to her own decisions the next?

She had to see Durant at least once. Were his parents living? Did he have sisters and brothers? Was the family in good health? Did the Durants have talents that might be passed on genetically? Her own parents had died relatively young, so she would be glad to hear that Cord Durant's were still alive.

Still, it seemed as if she were digging herself into a deeper hole by involving the man in her life, even on a strictly professional basis.

Abbie sighed heavily. It was done, whether she already regretted it or not. The appointment was set and she'd best keep it.

# Two

Abbie turned one way and then the other in front of her bedroom mirror, wondering if she looked any different. There were some slight physical changes beginning to take place in her body, tender breasts, for one, but nothing of her condition really showed, did it?

She had taken great care with her makeup and hair. Her blouse—which would show in the portrait—was a shade of teal that brought out the color of her eyes. Her slacks were teal, also, which was immaterial to the photo but necessary to a finished look.

It was crystal clear to her what she was doing: attempting to make the best possible impression today to eradicate the awful memory Cord Durant must have of how she had looked the morning she fled his condo.

Not that anything personal between them was an option at their impending meeting, but Abbie winced every time she remembered her appearance that morning. Makeup gone, hair flying, and wrinkled clothing—unquestionably the epitome of the "morning after."

The image repelled Abbie, as did the memory of her crude behavior. Pride demanded that Cord Durant see the person she really was, a habitually neat and stylish woman, a woman with poise and intelligence. He couldn't possibly have that impression of her at the present.

Despite satisfaction with her reflection in the mirror, Abbie's stomach was tied in knots. Her mental list of upcoming and necessary tasks was growing. Very soon now she would have to instigate a conversation with Bob Sidwell. Heaven only knew how he would take the news about his anchorwoman's condition. Friends would have to be told, curiosity about the baby's father deflected in the process, as she had no intention of imparting that information to anyone, except maybe for Sherry. That point wasn't yet settled in Abbie's mind. Sherry wasn't one to pass on private matters, but it might be best in the long run if no one knew.

A glance at the clock increased Abbie's tension; it was time to leave, if she was going to arrive at Durant's Studio at ten. Slipping into a teal-and-peach plaid jacket, she picked up her purse and took a final look in the mirror. She had used no perfume, which was unusual for her as she liked a light scent. But she wanted nothing about herself to suggest sensuality to Cord Durant.

Finally she left the house, got in her car and headed for the studio's area of town. She didn't want to arrive in a nervous state and forced calmness upon herself while she drove. A glance in the rearview mirror was reassuring: she looked as calm as if she were merely on her way to work.

Given her state of mind, looking calm was a small miracle. Talking to Cord Durant, figuring out what sort of man he was and learning something about his background was crucial to her peace of mind. At the same time, she had to avoid references to that night, convey indifference about it, if anything, and keep him totally in the dark about her real reason for contacting him. It was a tall order and would certainly stretch her acting ability.

Locating the studio took a little doing, as it was situated in an unfamiliar commercial area. Finally she spotted a nondescript sign, Durant Photography. The building was huge, but contained other businesses, Abbie saw by a number of other signs. Parking was no problem. Only three other cars occupied the ample lot, and Abbie wondered which one belonged to Durant.

Not that it mattered what kind of car he drove. His family ties mattered, his personality mattered, his health mattered, but not much else about the man was of any interest to her. Abbie sat in her car for a moment, nearly choking on an overfast heartbeat. She had set herself an awful task. If ever anyone had willingly walked into the lion's den, it was she. It was possible that Cord Durant had forgotten her and that night. This meeting could have some negative repercussions. If she weren't clever enough and he started adding things up...?

Abbie shivered and told herself to stop thinking the worst. This had to be done at whatever discomfort to herself. If she were ever going to meet with Cord, it had to be now, before her condition became obvious.

She walked into a vacant anteroom. It was plain, containing a desk with a telephone and several chairs. An inner door was ajar and from beyond it she heard, "Be with you in a minute!"

The voice was Cord Durant's. Abbie's stomach lurched sickeningly. She'd had very little trouble with nausea so far and blamed her rolling stomach now on the nerve-racking situation.

What if he thought she wanted to pick up where they had left off? Wouldn't that idea be any man's first thought, when a woman had been as easy as she had obviously been? She must be prepared to fend off anything personal from Durant.

Without replying to his remark, Abbie turned to a window and looked out. There was nothing to see other than the parking lot and the blank sides of several other barnlike commercial buildings. But she stood there because she didn't want to sit down.

"Abbie?"

She turned. Durant was in the doorway and a wave of discomfort reddened Abbie's cheeks. "Good morning."

Cord let his gaze sweep down to her teal pumps and back up to her face. She looked as fresh and clean as an April morning, and pretty, very pretty.

She also looked embarrassed again, which stopped the warmth he had intended greeting her with in his throat. "Your call surprised me," he said without a smile.

Thank God, she thought with intense relief. He was going to keep this businesslike. "I'm sure it did. But I need a new portrait."

There were dozens of portrait studios in Las Vegas. She hadn't had to come to him. Tactfully, Cord avoided pointing that out.

"Fine. Shall we get started?"

"Yes, thanks."

Cord stood aside and let her precede him through the door to the back of the building. Abbie passed within inches of him and despised the quickened beating of her heart while she did it. He was wearing faded jeans, sneakers and a white sweater with the sleeves pushed up. The sweater had a V neck, from which a swatch of dark hair protruded. He wore no jewelry, not even a watch.

She darted into a massive room and got out of Durant's way by stepping to the side of the door, which he left ajar. "We'll sit over there," he instructed, indicating several upholstered chairs around a low circular table.

Abbie crossed to the chairs and sat down. The room contained cameras and lights, two different arrangements of the equipment. One wall was a display gallery, apparently, as there were at least a dozen framed photographs hanging on it.

"I was just going to have a cup of coffee. Would you like one?" Cord said.

Her mouth felt sticky dry. "Yes, thank you."

He went behind a freestanding screen and came out a minute later with two cups. Silently, his expression closed, he brought one to her. Abbie took it and looked elsewhere, anywhere but into his eyes, which were, she'd seen, a true, unabashed blue.

But with his back turned briefly while he skirted the round table and went to a chair, Abbie sneaked a look at his broad shoulders and nearly black hair. She had touched that hair, she knew, run her fingers through it. The memory wasn't distinct, more like sensation than fact, but it had happened, all the same.

She took a sip of coffee while Cord seated himself, blocking out memory, such as it was, and concentrating on keeping her hands steady. "What type of portrait do you need?" he asked.

"Type? I'm not sure I understand. A portrait is a portrait, isn't it?"

Cord sat back, struck by the fact that she didn't know his reputation. So why then had she come to him? People didn't pay his fees unless they wanted something special. Ordinary portraits were inexpensive; a Durant was not.

He pushed the topic of fees aside. Abbie Forbes had a reason for this meeting, and it wasn't to get her picture taken. After nearly two months of total silence, this sudden contact was extremely suspect.

"Do you need it for business?" he persisted.

"I work for KSTV," Abbie said. "The station is always involved in promotions of one sort or another and portraits are necessary."

"I know where you work. I've seen your broadcast."

"Oh, yes, of course." Abbie looked down at her coffee cup. "Well, that's the type of portrait I need, something for...promotions."

"Serious, then? Or smiling?"

"Hmm...probably smiling."

"Your clothing is fine. The color is good for you."

He was scrutinizing her much too closely, making her edgy. Was he thinking about that night? Remembering, when she could not?

Oh, God, what had taken place in his condo? Had she participated eagerly? She had wondered about that so often. Other than the first few months of her marriage, her entire sex life could be categorized as a dismal failure. She had never been particularly comfortable with men on a personal level until Nick, and she'd fallen very hard for him. His illness and death had drained her of desire, or so she had believed.

But this man sitting across from her had reached her during a vulnerable moment, and it made her want to shriek because she couldn't remember it.

It was disconcerting to realize that Cord Durant was an unusually handsome man, a compelling man, and to recognize within herself a strange, unfamiliar response to his aura. She sat straighter, a little more rigidly, denying the sensation.

He got up abruptly and went behind the screen, returning with a box of doughnuts and some paper napkins, which he placed on the table. "Help yourself," he said while dunking a doughnut into his coffee.

Abbie had eaten an orange for breakfast and preferred getting this appointment over and done with. But she had to prolong things until she could steer the conversation to Durant, so she took a doughnut and a napkin.

"Tell me something about yourself," Cord said after a bite of soggy doughnut.

Abbie's eyes widened. She'd had portraits done many times throughout her career and none of the photographers had requested personal information.

"I want to capture the real Abbie Forbes," Cord explained.

She laughed, nervously. "You're looking at her."

"What I'm looking at is an attractive but uptight woman," Cord rebutted. "That's what the camera will portray. I think there's a lot more to you than what I'm seeing right now."

Abbie broke off a piece of her doughnut and brought it to her mouth, attempting a sophistication she was far from feeling. "You're referring to... Perhaps we should clear the air about that night, Mr. Durant."

"Cord," he said sharply, annoyed that she would attempt formality when she had writhed beneath him and demanded, adorably and seductively, everything he'd had to give.

"Cord," she echoed uneasily, unable to meet his eyes. "I knew this would be difficult, but..."

"But you came here anyway."

"I needed a new portrait."

*Which you could have gotten from a dozen different studios! Why, really, are you here, Abbie? What is it you're looking for from me?*

Cord said none of it. That harried expression he'd been picking up in her eyes during her news broadcasts was more pronounced in person. She was trying very hard to appear nonplussed, but she looked as uncomfortable as any person he'd ever seen.

He decided to play along. Sooner or later whatever was bothering her would come out. It had to do with him or she never would have called.

"We don't have to clear the air on anything, unless you want to," he said quietly. "I gave you my number, you didn't use it. End of subject."

Abbie drew a nervous breath. "I appreciate your attitude."

His attitude was that he'd like to go over to her, grab her by the shoulders and rid her of that determined wariness. Did she think that night meant nothing to him? Good Lord, did it mean nothing to her?

Confused, Cord returned to business. "What I try to do," he said a trifle raggedly, "is to capture a subject's inner qualities."

"Oh, I don't think I need anything like that." Abbie's eyes went to the wall of photographs, which were too far away to see with any distinction. But she was beginning to catch on that Cord Durant wasn't merely another photographer. "Just an ordinary pose is fine," she added.

"Nothing about you is ordinary," Cord said softly.

Abbie's head jerked around. Color flooded her face.

But it was best to let such a remark pass, and she straightened her shoulders. "Maybe you should tell me something about Cord Durant. Apparently your technique is different than I expected."

"My technique?"

The flush deepened in Abbie's cheeks. "Your photographic technique!"

"Naturally," Cord muttered impolitely.

Abbie set her cup and the remains of her doughnut on the table and got up. Without looking at Durant she walked over to the wall of photographs. At first her gaze didn't really focus. Her stomach had started acting up something fierce, probably from that greasy doughnut, and she slowly drew in several deep breaths, willing the woozy feeling to vanish.

Then she began to see the framed pictures. There was beauty in each of them, but there was something else as well, something intangible that set them apart from portraits she'd seen before. Some of the faces were famous. "You photograph stars?"

Cord came up behind her. "Some," he admitted. "I have a studio in Los Angeles, too. A lot of these were taken right here in Vegas, though."

"They're . . ." Abbie searched for the right word and settled for "wonderful." But she was certain now that Cord Durant was a master of portrait photography. These weren't just faces, they were personalities.

She had to sit down again, swallowing hard in an attempt to forestall the nausea in her midsection. Getting to the point of this meeting was becoming critical; she might have to make a quick exit. "Do you have any family?"

"Family?" The question struck Cord as weird, and he frowned as he resumed his chair.

"Yes, family," Abbie confirmed somewhat breathlessly. She couldn't be sick now, she just couldn't be!

"I have an older brother who's a career officer in the Marine Corps," Cord said cautiously. "Why?"

"Your parents?"

"Both dead."

"Oh . . . I'm sorry."

"They died in a plane crash when I was thirteen. My brother took over with my care."

"Oh." Abbie's spirit brightened slightly. She licked her lips and again willed the nausea away.

"Do you have family?" Cord didn't know why he was asking, but for some inexplicable reason Abbie seemed interested in discussing families.

"No . . . none," she whispered and stumbled to her feet. "Do you have a bathroom?"

"Behind the screen." Cord stood up while she ran across the room and disappeared behind the screen. "What in hell's going on here?" he mumbled.

The large high-ceilinged building was full of echoes, and even Abbie running water into the bathroom sink couldn't conceal what was happening in there. Cord stood there, frozen for a long moment, mystified by this whole episode.

And then, like a bolt of lightning, things started adding up. Why she'd contacted him after—he added up time— seven weeks of strict avoidance; why she'd asked about his family. She was pregnant...and she wouldn't be here if she didn't think...believe...*know* that the baby was his.

Cord felt a little like heaving himself. His knees actually got weak, and he wasn't ordinarily a man who reacted to shock so physically.

But this wasn't just any shock. He sat down, but bobbed back up to his feet. Pacing then, he raked his fingers through his hair. He had to be wrong, he silently argued, and felt immeasurably better when he remembered using a condom.

But not the first time. They had made love twice, and the first time had been so wild he hadn't even thought of protection.

Cord started for the screen, frantic again, but stopped himself from pounding on the bathroom door. The water was still running, although Abbie's misery had ceased.

He strode around the studio, more upset than he could ever remember being. Why hadn't she said right out, *I'm pregnant and you're the father?* Instead, she'd sneaked in here pretending to need a portrait. Why? What was going on with her?

Hearing the bathroom door opening, Cord did his best to compose himself. His heart was thumping like a crazy thing, but he'd give Abbie every chance to explain.

She was pale, he saw, as she rounded the screen.

"I'm terribly sorry," she said huskily, not quite meeting his eyes. "Let's forget the photograph. I really have to leave." Abbie went to where she'd been sitting and picked up her purse. "Sorry I intruded on your weekend."

Cord couldn't believe what he was hearing. Did she think he was going to let her walk out of here without some conversation?

"Do you want to make an appointment for another day?" he asked coolly.

Abbie was sidling toward the door. "No...no, I think not. I'll call."

Cord followed her to the front office, his jaw clenched, his eyes narrowed. Abbie Forbes had to think he was just plain stupid, he thought angrily as she walked to the outer door.

"Maybe you've got the flu," he said coldly.

Abbie stopped with her hand on the door. "Possibly. Something always seems to be going around. Thanks for your time."

"Then again," Cord said with barely controlled fury, "you could be pregnant."

"What did you say?" Abbie turned, paler suddenly by several shades.

"You heard what I said." Scowling, Cord advanced. "Don't underestimate my intelligence, Abbie. I can add two and two as well as you can."

"But why would you think...?" Abbie stammered. "Besides, if I were...expecting a child, it wouldn't be any of your business." She ardently hoped that her expression was careless. If she could possibly drum up a laugh, it would be very effective at this ghastly moment.

"You came here for a reason, and it sure wasn't to get your picture taken," Cord said harshly, practically in her face.

"That's absurd. I wanted a good photographer and..."

"You didn't know if I was good, bad or otherwise," Cord retorted.

"Of course I knew!" Abbie lied. "You've got an incredible imagination, apparently. Goodbye." Sidestepping, she reached for the door handle.

But a big hand came around her and slapped the door closed. "You're not leaving until I get some answers that make sense," Cord snarled.

His anger fired her own, and Abbie whirled. "I happen to be feeling ill, Mr. Durant. I'd like to leave!"

"Mr. Durant! What the hell's wrong with you, lady? If I'm confused, it's no damned wonder! One night seven weeks ago you were all over me, then acted the next morning like I had something contagious. After that there was nothing, not a word, and suddenly you decide you need a photo and call me? Likely story, Abbie. You knew nothing about my work when you walked in here, and what's more, you didn't give a damn if I even knew which end of a camera was up. You asked about my family, for God's sake, not whether or not I could take a decent photograph! Come off it, Abbie. I wasn't born yesterday."

The jig was up and Abbie knew it. She could hold her ground and insist that he was being ridiculous, but what about later? If he'd added two and two so well from only a few clues, what would he come up with when word got around that Abbie Forbes was indeed pregnant?

"I didn't come here to involve you in my...situation," she said hoarsely.

"No? Why, then?"

"I merely wanted some facts about your background."

"And you didn't think I'd figure it out?" Cord walked away, fingering his hair into a mess. "You must have thought I was completely dense."

"I thought no such thing! For your information, I barely thought of you at all!"

Cord turned, one eyebrow cocked. "Until you found out you were pregnant. You weren't going to tell me, were you?"

Abbie's color changed from pale to hot pink. None of this conversation had been anticipated and she didn't like it in the least. "I want nothing from you, not one single thing."

Cord folded his arms. "Maybe I want something different."

"You have nothing to say about it!"

"That's where you're wrong, honey."

He'd spoken sarcastically, annoying Abbie to anger. "I'm not going to stand here and argue with you."

"Then talk to me," Cord snapped. "Because we are going to communicate on some level. I'm willing to discuss this sensibly. Anger isn't going to get us anywhere."

"Oh?" Abbie retorted. "I suppose I'm the only one angry here?"

Cord hesitated, then nodded. "You're right. I apologize for blowing my top. I just couldn't believe you'd walk out of here without a word."

Abbie slumped against a wall. "If I hadn't gotten sick you never would have guessed."

"That's not true. I suspected something funny when Danny told me you'd called for an appointment. Abbie, why didn't you call before? I thought about contacting you many times, but you were so embarrassed that morning, and remembering how you ran always stopped me."

"I was humiliated, not merely embarrassed," Abbie said low, with her eyes down. "I'd never done anything so... so..."

"So human?" Cord questioned softly.

Her eyes rose to his. "Reckless is a better word," she said coldly, and pushed herself away from the wall. "Are you going to stop me from leaving?"

"Will you see me again? This isn't over, Abbie."

"No," she agreed wearily. "It's not over. Apparently you intend to interfere, whatever I say about it."

Cord's mouth tightened. "If that's the way you prefer putting it, yes, I intend to interfere. Name our next meeting, I'll leave that up to you. I'd settle for dinner together tonight, if you agree."

The idea of the two of them sitting down to eat together made Abbie's stomach protest. "Not dinner."

"Then what? I'm not fond of ultimatums, Abbie, but if you don't willingly see me again, I'll come to the station."

Abbie's breath caught. "You wouldn't!"

A gleam entered Cord's eyes. "No one else knows yet, do they?"

"And I'd like to keep it like that for a while yet," Abbie snapped. "I do have my job to consider, you know."

"You also have a baby to consider," Cord shot back.

Abbie's eyes seethed. "Don't you dare preach to me. Coming here was the biggest mistake of my life. The *second* biggest mistake," she amended.

"If you feel that way, why are you keeping the baby?"

"Because . . . because . . . oh, I don't have to explain anything to you! There's a park at Pecos and Sunset. I'll be there at two tomorrow afternoon."

"Fine! I'll be there, too."

He watched her yank open the door and dart through it, and her exit was almost as hurried and unnerving as it had been that morning in his condo. At the window he watched her get into her car and back it out of its parking space. When the parking area was empty, he remained at the window and faced how shaken he was by the past few minutes.

He didn't doubt that Abbie's baby was his. She never would have come here if it weren't. He believed that she merely wanted some information about him and had hoped to gather it while keeping him in the dark.

Her plan had gone awry. Maybe fate had intervened. She wasn't an accomplished liar and her whole act had been a shallow cover-up.

Cord's thoughts went back in time, to a thirteen-year-old boy who had lost both parents in one tragic accident. To his brother, Gary, who'd done his best to make up for the enormous loss. To the boy again, who'd never stopped missing his parents, especially his father, who had played baseball with him and taken him fishing and listened to everything the boy had had to say.

A baby, a child. *His* baby, *his* child. Oh, yes, he fully intended to interfere, by legal measures if necessary. He would do whatever it took; he was not going to walk away from his own flesh and blood.

# Three

"**I** need to know something," Abbie said, speaking coolly, because it was either coolness or rage with Cord Durant. She resented everything about the man, his good looks, his unflappable determination to intrude, even the expensive car in which he'd arrived at Sunset Park.

"Ask me anything," Cord replied. They were sitting in the third row of a set of bleachers. A group of boys was tossing softballs around, warming up for a game. The bleachers were dotted with onlookers, families of the young athletes, apparently. Abbie had chosen the meeting place, and it seemed slightly ironic to Cord that she would inadvertently lead him to a boy's ball game when his own thoughts had recently taken him to just such outings in his past.

"Why haven't you suggested that the baby isn't yours?"

Cord turned his head to look at the woman at his side. She was keeping plenty of empty space between them, making sure, he was positive, that they didn't touch.

"You never would have contacted me if it wasn't," he said evenly.

Abbie looked away, angry that he would be so logical. "What do you intend to do?"

They were both dressed casually, wearing similar garb, sweat suits and sneakers, fitting in with everyone else at the park as if they were there merely to enjoy the sunshine and the fun of a youngsters' ball game.

Cord spoke quietly. "What do you intend to do?"

"Can't you give me a straight answer?"

He studied her profile, her small nose, the perfection of her complexion, the sensual swell of her upper lip, her long lashes, and a word popped into his mind: *Luxuriant*. On television Abbie Forbes was elegantly attractive; in person she was startlingly beautiful.

"Are we going to spend this meeting snapping at each other, Abbie?"

She closed her eyes and tried to calm herself. She'd been waspish since the previous morning, scared spitless, too on edge to settle into a normal weekend routine. Last night had passed slowly and miserably, taken up with alternating bouts of self-anger because she'd been so stupid and worried about Durant's intentions.

She got up abruptly. "I'm going for a walk."

Cord sat there for a few seconds, then stood up and followed with a sigh of impatience. He stayed several steps behind her until they were away from the bleachers, then drawled, "You must either be feeling a whole lot better or in training for the three-minute mile."

Abbie slowed her furious pace. Cord fell into step beside her. "There's no reason for us to bicker, Abbie. We're in this together and we might as well make the best of it."

"I'll make the best of it when I hear what kind of trouble you're planning to stir up."

Cord grabbed her by the arm, bringing them both to a halt. "I'll only make trouble if you try to keep me away from my child," he said flatly. "Do I make myself clear?"

She stared into his darkened eyes and saw intractable determination. But she was burning with the same emotion. "I'll fight you, Cord, and I'm not without influence in this town. Do I make *myself* clear?"

His hand tightened on her arm. "Why do we have to be on opposite sides? I'm willing to cooperate with any sensible plan. Why can't you?"

"What sensible plan?" she asked suspiciously.

"I've been thinking about co-guardianship."

"Co...? Not on your life!" Jerking her arm free, Abbie stalked off.

If she weren't pregnant, Cord knew that he'd tackle her and bring her to the ground. Never had a woman infuriated him the way Abbie had just done.

"There are a few other options," Cord called, deciding to lay it on her without any more soft soap. He'd spent the previous day and most of the night thinking about the situation from every conceivable angle. An amicable agreement for equal guardianship would keep everything peaceful, but Abbie had discarded that idea without even thinking about it.

Well, she was in for a rude awakening. He stood where he was and waited for her to turn around and walk back to him. "What options?" she questioned.

"Maybe we should sit down. There's a picnic table over there."

Abbie marched to the table, ignoring the man at her side. They chose opposite benches and ended up facing each other.

Cord looked her right in the eye. "We have three options, as I see it. One, the execution of a legal document detailing co-guardianship. Two, a court battle, which I assure you would take place. Or three, we could get married."

"We could what?"

"Get married. Temporarily, of course. The baby would have my name, which it could have even without marriage if you agreed, *which* I doubt you'd do without legal pressure, and the community would think everything was peaches and cream with us, which would give the baby a good start in life. You wouldn't have to explain anything to anyone, particularly your employer. My condition is that there wouldn't be any kind of legal hassle during the divorce over equal custody."

There was no friendliness in Cord's eyes. He was deadly serious and wanted Abbie to know it. "Let's talk about our number-two option. I'll take you to court, Abbie. I'll raise such a stink this town will remember it for years. KSTV loves publicity, but the powers-that-be won't like their favorite anchorperson's face and name plastered across the headlines in this instance, I can guarantee you."

Abbie was trembling. "You're the most disgusting person I've ever met."

"You didn't think I was at all disgusting one night in December, if I remember correctly. But you have your own memories of that night. I don't need to spell anything out, do I?"

She was too humiliated to admit that she remembered nothing beyond a few kisses. If she did, he'd probably be crude enough to give her details.

"Maybe I have a few options of my own," she said weakly, vowing not to shed tears no matter how horrible this got.

"Lay them on me," Cord replied. "I'm listening."

Abbie's mind raced, but there was only one thing she wanted, and that was for Cord Durant to disappear from the face of the earth.

That wasn't going to happen. He was big and healthy and as mean as rat poison. Her career wouldn't withstand a sensational court battle, which he had to know. The thought of giving him, a total stranger, equal guardianship of her unborn child was abhorrent. Visualizing marriage with a man she barely knew made her sick to her stomach.

Why, dear God, had meeting him again, talking to him, seemed so crucial? He'd known nothing. She had caused this herself. What kind of fool had she become?

"I'm waiting," Cord said.

Abbie looked at him across the picnic table and despised herself for thinking him handsome even now. Good looks were so trivial in comparison to real-life problems. What did thick, dark hair and a magnificent mouth matter, when they belonged to a man without a drop of compassion?

"I have no options, which you well know," she said raggedly. "If I hadn't been so naive and contacted you, you never would have known about the baby."

"You could have learned all about my background without contacting me, Abbie. I belong to several well-known photographers' organizations, and my vital statistics are available to anyone who's interested."

Stunned, Abbie stared at him. How could she have been so remiss?

"Maybe you wanted me to know," Cord said softly. "Abbie, that night was . . ."

"Don't!" she cried and struggled to her feet. "I *didn't* want you to know! I blundered badly in calling you, but I had no ulterior motives, believe me. I'll live with the results, make no mistake, but I . . . I need some time to sort it out."

Cord rose slowly. "Give me your home telephone number. I tried to get it through information and found out it's unlisted."

"I don't want you to have it."

"Do you want me calling the station? Abbie, listen to me. I'm not playing games. If I don't hear from you in a matter of days, I'm going to see my attorney."

Abbie was shaking. "You . . . you bastard," she whispered.

"Call me any name you want. It changes nothing. What's your home number?"

She gave it, quickly, and walked away, leaving him to stare after her. He said then, under his breath, "It doesn't have to be this way, Abbie. It doesn't have to be this way at all."


Cord called on Monday evening. "How are you feeling?"

"Fine."

"Have you come to a decision yet?"

"No." Abbie slammed the phone down so hard she marveled that it survived the blast.

Cord called on Tuesday evening. "Don't hang up on me tonight, Abbie. I'm going to L.A. in the morning and will be back in Vegas on Thursday. I want your answer then."

"On Thursday," Abbie said in a saccharine tone. "You're very good at throwing your weight around, aren't you? You know, I've been doing some thinking, and the publicity of a court battle wouldn't do your career any good either."

Cord laughed softly. "Believe me, honey, a court battle could drag on for months and not hurt my career an iota. Thursday, Abbie. I think we should get together for the big event. Where do you suggest, your place or mine?"

"You'll never step one foot in my house!"

"Then mine. You know the address. What time should I expect you?"

"I will not go to your condo," Abbie said furiously, enunciating each syllable with abnormal distinction.

Every speck of warmth left Cord's voice. "Where, then?"

She was trapped into another decision when she hadn't even made the first one, and realized that she didn't want to take this fiasco public. Not yet.

But she didn't want Cord Durant in her neighborhood, let alone in her house. "All right, I'll come to your place! I'll be there at . . . at . . . ten."

"So late?"

"I have a meeting on Thursday evening. It should be over around nine-thirty."

"All right, fine. See you then."

They hung up without goodbyes.

Abbie glared at the instrument for a moment then went to the west window. Sherry's lights were on, so she was home. Stewing, Abbie debated a talk with her good friend, which she'd been considering on and off since Saturday. She needed to talk to someone as she was getting nowhere with the decision on her own. Cord's options never left her mind, affecting even her work. Bob Sidwell had asked her only today if something was bothering her.

She'd lied and said no, that everything was great.

But everything wasn't great. She was pregnant and alone and scared witless. A legal battle or a marriage made in hell, those were really her only choices. Certainly she couldn't sign anything giving Cord Durant or any other stranger equal custody of her child. That's all the man was to her, a stranger. Didn't he realize that?

But, of course, he didn't. He had no idea that the sum total of her memories of the two of them consisted of some champagne-dulled laughs, dances and kisses.

Swiftly then, before she could change her mind, Abbie dashed out her front door, crossed the stretch of lawn between the two houses and rapped on Sherry's door. Footsteps resounded from within and Abbie knew her friend's habits: Sherry was looking through the peephole.

The door opened immediately. "Hi, Ab, come on in. How ya doing?"

"Not so good."

Sherry was a pretty brunette. Her features instantly radiated concern. "What's wrong?"

Abbie sighed. "I need to talk to someone about a major problem."

Sherry drew her into the house and closed the door. "Let's go to the kitchen. I'll put on a pot of coffee."

"No coffee for me, thanks. It doesn't sit well these days. I...I'm pregnant, Sherry."

The woman stopped dead in her tracks. "You're what?"

Abbie's hands rose to cover her face. "Oh, God, what am I going to do?" She felt Sherry's arms slide around her.

"Come to the living room and sit down, Ab." She led Abbie to a comfortable chair. "Do you want anything, a cup of tea, maybe?"

"Nothing, thanks. Sherry, I've kept this bottled up for two weeks and it's killing me."

"I can see that." Sherry sat in a nearby chair. "Abbie, I didn't know you were dating anyone."

"I wasn't. I'm not." Abbie threw her head back. "That's what's so awful, I didn't—*don't*—know the...father. I met him at a Christmas party. Sherry, I honestly don't know what happened. I was exhausted, I remember that, and I'd had a dental appointment that afternoon. I probably shouldn't even mention that because I really don't know if it had anything to do with my blacking out. But I drank some champagne and suddenly there was this man, Cord

Durant. We danced together, I remember laughing at his jokes, and from then on things get really patchy." Abbie groaned. "This sounds like a fairy tale."

"It sounds like you met a man you liked. There's nothing so terrible about that, Abbie."

"There's nothing wrong with meeting a man and ending up in his bed, all in one night? It sounds plenty wrong to me, Sherry. I didn't even do things like that when I was in college and most of my friends were playing musical beds!"

"I know you didn't, Ab."

"Sherry, the next thing I knew I was waking up in a strange bed. Between some very vague kisses and the next morning, everything is a complete blank. Two weeks ago I went to the doctor. I'm pregnant. The baby is due in September."

Sherry drew in a long, slow breath. "I...I'm slightly shell-shocked, Ab."

"That's not the worst of it. I began wondering what kind of man Cord Durant was. The little I remembered about him consisted solely of jokes, laughter and champagne bubbles. I wondered about his family...you know the sort of stuff.

"Anyway, I called his studio. Oh, did I mention that he's a photographer?"

Sherry became very still. "I think I've heard of him, Abbie."

"Really?"

"Yes, through the bank. What was it...?" Sherry's expression became thoughtful. "I know what it was! Cord Durant's considered to be one of the best portrait photographers in the business!"

"Oh, Lord, why didn't I talk to you right away?" Abbie moaned. "Well, let me tell you something, Sherry. Durant might know his way around a camera, but he's the biggest horse's patoot that ever drew breath."

"You told him about the baby and he refused responsibility," Sherry said flatly.

"Don't I wish? I told him nothing. I made an appointment to have a portrait made, just so I could meet him without appearing interested in him personally. All I wanted was to see him just once, to talk to him a little." Abbie put her head back again. "Everything went wrong. I was so blasted nervous and I ate part of a doughnut and drank some coffee. Before I realized what was happening, I got sick and had to run for the bathroom. Durant must have some sort of sixth sense, because he figured it all out while I was in there being sick and trying to keep it silent.

"He gave me three options. I can either give him equal guardianship, we can go to court and fight it out or... get this one, Sherry... or I can marry him on a temporary basis so he'll have legal rights to his child. Oh, yes, should I choose his third option, I have to promise him—probably in writing—that I won't fight equal custody of the child during our divorce."

Sherry was about to say something when Abbie added, "One more thing. He's given me until Thursday to make up my mind."

"Well," Sherry finally said, obviously stunned.

"Yes, well," Abbie repeated dully.

They sat there silently, looking at each other. Abbie pulled a tissue from her pocket and wiped the corners of her eyes. "I don't know what to do. A court battle, which he's threatened to make as public and sensational as he can, will destroy my career. He knows it, too."

Sherry cleared her throat. "I guess that leaves the other two options."

"I cannot give a total stranger partial custody of my child. Sherry, the baby is becoming real to me. I always wanted children, you know that." Abbie laid a hand on her lower abdomen. "I'm not unhappy about the baby. It was a shock, of course, but deep down I'm so elated I can't see straight."

"Do you believe Durant will follow through with his threats?" Sherry asked.

Abbie's expression turned bitter. "You bet I do. That man has absolutely no heart. Why would he want the baby? He's only throwing his weight around to... to stroke his own damned ego."

"Well... I doubt that anyone would cause so much trouble without good reason, Ab. No one likes going to court."

"There are people who drum up false suits at the drop of a hat."

"For money, Abbie. Durant didn't hint at wanting money from you, did he?"

Abbie sat up straighter. "No, he didn't," she said slowly. "But do you suppose that's what's in the back of his mind? Maybe he sees this as an opportunity for a little blackmail."

"I suppose it's possible," Sherry speculated. "You could ask him point-blank about it. But I think you should be prepared in case he laughs in your face, or worse, gets mad. You've virtually eliminated complying with two of his options, which leaves marrying him. You said he indicated a temporary arrangement, which would give you time to get to know him. Your career wouldn't be hurt by a quiet divorce, Abbie, and maybe you wouldn't object to partial custody if you really knew Durant."

"I doubt that," Abbie said gloomily.

"Then take your chances in court."

"I can see the headlines now," Abbie said huskily, her eyes tearing again. "'Unmarried Anchorwoman Sued For Custody Of Her Unborn Child.'"

"It would make the news, all right," Sherry agreed dryly.

Abbie wiped her eyes. "I can't believe this is happening. I haven't even looked at another man since Nick died."

"Did Durant question you about other men?"

"No, which I have to admit surprised me. When I mentioned it to him he said he knew I never would have contacted him if the baby wasn't his. It's the truth, but why would he be so willing to believe in my good reputation?"

"Very good question, Abbie. Maybe the man's not as bad as you think. Look at it from his standpoint. Maybe he's always wanted children, too. If he truly wants his baby, wouldn't he use every possible weapon to get it? You would, why wouldn't he?"

"He doesn't deserve to have custody. What did he do but have himself a good time one cold night in December?"

"Having a good time is the only role a man has in the childbearing process, unless a woman allows more, Ab," Sherry gently reminded.

Abbie's passion faded. "Sorry I got so carried away. I really appreciate your letting me cry on your shoulder." She sighed. "I'm just so mixed up."

Sherry got to her feet. "I'm going to make a pot of herbal tea, which I guarantee won't irritate your stomach. You sit there and unwind. I'll only be a few minutes."

Abbie was glad she'd told Sherry everything, but had baring her soul accomplished anything beyond relieving some of the pressure she'd been living with? She didn't believe Cord wanted money from her, although out-and-out blackmail would almost be easier to deal with than the truth. He wanted his baby. Damn his hide, he wanted *her* baby!

She was up and walking the floor when Sherry returned with a teapot and two cups. "He's forcing me into a phony marriage," she said bitterly. "It's ridiculous and . . . and repugnant, but what else can I do? Can you imagine what Ron Harrison would do if he got wind of my situation?"

"*When* he gets wind of it, Abbie. Impending motherhood can be kept quiet for only so long." Sherry held up a cup. "Sit down and drink your tea. It'll make you feel better."

They sat and sipped and talked in quieter tones. "I can't sign a piece of paper giving him co-custody of my baby," Abbie said again.

"You have to get to know him," Sherry agreed. "The whole thing would be over in a year, Abbie."

"But then he'll have as much to say about the baby as I will."

"I don't see that you have a choice. Not if you want to keep your career moving in an upward direction."

They refilled their cups. "He has a studio in Los Angeles, too," Abbie stated.

"If he's the Cord Durant I've heard about, then he's really very successful. Try to find a bright side. Every child deserves to know his father. Wouldn't a man who'd fought so hard for parental rights be a good and loving father?"

"I wish I could remember that night," Abbie said wistfully. "He hinted that it was something special, inferring right afterward that I had my own memories and he didn't have to spell out anything."

"So he doesn't know that the night is a blank for you?"

"I was too humiliated to talk about it."

"Maybe you should tell him," Sherry suggested.

"How can I carry on a normal conversation with a man who's threatening my very existence?" Abbie sighed. "Sorry if I sound self-pitying, but this has had me going in circles for weeks now. Since December, really. I'll never understand what happened if I live to be 150."

Abbie glanced at her watch. "It's getting late and we both have to be up in the morning." She stood up. "Thanks for listening, Sherry."

"Anytime, pal." Sherry walked to the front door with her friend. "Have you decided, then? About marrying him?"

"It seems impossible, doesn't it? Forced marriages don't happen in this day and age."

"Not every day, they don't," Sherry replied with a small smile. "Keep your chin up, Ab. Durant might have the upper hand right now, but you're a lot tougher than he knows. You went through hell with Nick and survived. You'll survive this, too."

Abbie stood in the open doorway a moment, then squared her shoulders. "I'll have to try, won't I? Good night, Sherry."

"Let me know what happens."

"I will. Thanks again."

Abbie slept better that night and performed at work the next day with more of her usual efficiency. On Thursday morning she faced herself in the bathroom mirror. The one person in this mess who deserved none of it was her baby, and he or she was not going to be tossed back and forth between fighting parents like some kind of toy. If it took a loveless marriage to assure her baby a decent future, she would do it.

In the process, however, Cord Durant was going to understand what *she* expected from the union. She might be stymied as far as options went, but that's where her confusion stopped.

All of which she would explain in no uncertain terms tonight.

# Four

The lobby of Cord's building had marble floors, Abbie noted while waiting for him to answer the security telephone. He came on the line. "Abbie?"

"I'm in the lobby."

"I'll buzz down to open the elevator doors."

"Thank you." Abbie hung the phone on its wall hook. Almost immediately a set of elevator doors opened with a pleasant-sounding *ding!*

She stepped in and pushed number five. Being backed into a corner wasn't something Abbie's normally good nature took lightly, and returning to the scene of the crime, so to speak, was a lot more daunting than she'd imagined it would be. Her hasty exit from Cord's building that December morning had precluded any appreciation of the lobby's excellent Italian marble, for instance, and what exactly was she going to see in the man's condo that also eluded memory? It was all unnerving, every single aspect of the fiasco in which she found herself floundering.

What was that remark Cord had made about her "being all over him" that night? Abbie's lips pursed. Surely he'd exaggerated. She'd never been "all over" a man in her life!

The elevator made a speedy and nearly silent ascent to the fifth floor. Abbie stepped out and headed, unerringly, to Cord's door, grateful that she at least remembered that small detail.

The door opened before she could ring the bell. Cord stood there, his eyes dark and unfathomable. "Hello."

"Hello."

Cord moved aside. "Come in."

"Thank you." Abbie swept past him, but stopped at once. A foyer...yes, she remembered the foyer now.

"Go on in to the living room," Cord told her.

She took a few tentative steps beyond the foyer's archway. The living room was a medley of off whites, beiges and browns in an L-shaped pattern that connected with a formal dining room. Beyond that area's furniture placement was a set of sliding glass doors, opening, Abbie remembered, onto a balcony. Everything was very appealing. Professionally decorated, she was positive. Also, it was vaguely familiar. Her gaze rapidly moved over furniture, carpet and decorator pieces, landing, to her intense dismay, on a set of ornate double doors, doors which she knew led to his bedroom!

"Would you like to take off your jacket?" Cord inquired.

Abbie's jacket was lined and too warm for inside wear. "Yes, thanks." Shrugging from the jacket, Abbie handed it to Cord.

"Sit down." He left with the jacket. Abbie gingerly lowered herself to the cushion of an overstuffed chair covered in a nubby oatmeal-colored fabric. She was scanning the room when Cord returned.

"Can I get you something to drink?"

"No, thank you."

Cord chose the sofa. He leaned forward, his arms resting on his knees, his hands dangling in between. Abbie's gaze darted to him and then away, but the glance had been enough to know that he was wearing jeans and a navy blue sweater. She still had on her working clothes, having gone directly from her broadcast to a meeting and then here. Her outfit was a smartly styled gray business suit and a plum-colored silk blouse.

"I like the way you dress," Cord said, startling her.

"Uh . . . thanks."

"Don't be uncomfortable. I'm not nearly the ogre you think I am."

She arched a dubious eyebrow. "We probably shouldn't get into that debate."

Cord sat back. "Tell me what's so wrong about a man wanting to be a father to his son or daughter?"

"I'd just as soon not discuss ethics, either, if you don't mind."

"You prefer getting right to the point."

"It's why I'm here," Abbie reminded flatly.

"All right, I'm listening," Cord said quietly. He appeared relaxed, by effort, but was internally keyed up. He'd never given much thought to children, relegating such ideas to the future. It seemed strange that the future had arrived prematurely and forever united him and Abbie Forbes. But their carelessness was not going to hurt his—*their*—child's chances.

Besides, he liked Abbie. A lot. Maybe his feelings even went beyond liking, or they could if she ever got close to again becoming the woman she'd been the night they met. That woman had been special. He could see her in the one sitting so primly in his living room, if he tried hard enough.

Abbie inhaled slowly. Admitting total defeat went against the grain. Only one factor made this little chat slightly palatable: once past it, her nerves might settle down.

"I concede to your . . . third option," she said without looking at him.

Cord's heart skipped a beat. "Marriage?"

"With conditions."

"Being?" Cord questioned with a slightly cocked eyebrow when she didn't immediately plunge into her terms.

"A definite time limit on the length of the arrangement and a prenuptial agreement on finances. During the marriage, you pay your expenses, I'll pay mine. Our incomes are not to be mingled, nor any assets we now possess. During the divorce we'll make no financial claims on each other and will agree to share the support of our child.''

"Agreed."

Abbie lifted her chin. "Separate bedrooms."

Cord cleared his throat. "Agreed."

"We'll live in my house, or appear to. You, of course, may come and go as you please.''

"Anything else?"

"A private ceremony."

Cord got up and walked around the room. He stopped suddenly and faced her. "How private?"

"A trip to city hall should do it," Abbie said coolly.

Cord circled the room again. Furtively Abbie watched, wondering why that condition should bother him.

But it did. Cord stood with his hands on his hips and declared flatly, "I don't like it."

"Well, I don't particularly give a damn. If you think that you and I are going to have some sort of splashy wedding, think again."

Cord stood his ground. "And if *you* think we're sneaking off like two thieves in the night, *you* think again. I don't happen to be ashamed of our relationship, or of its result. I want my brother to be there, and my friends. And you might think about this, too. Our marriage is going to get some publicity, whether you like it or not, and a ceremony at city hall just isn't good enough."

His logic, Abbie was beginning to realize, was usually too sound to dispute, irritating or not. It wouldn't matter who she married at this stage of her career, the event was going to draw some public notice.

But this wedding was going to be such a farce, a mockery of the solemnity of every loving couple's marriage vows. She felt like a fool sitting there and planning both the inception and death of a union that was nothing more than a contractual agreement.

She felt more than foolish, Abbie realized. Sadness, too, was present in her system. She hadn't thought of remarrying again in precise terms, but in the back of her mind was a vague hope of someday finding another Nick. Cord Durant was not him. Cord was pushy and demanding and not very pleasant. The unrecalled emotions and feelings that had driven her to his bed that night in December had apparently vanished with the morning light and a clear head, and she was truly finding it difficult even to be civil to the man.

Abbie got up from the nubby chair and went beyond the dining-room table to the glass sliders, where she stood with her back to Cord. "I'm not accustomed to being told when to jump *and* how high," she said resentfully.

"I'm not accustomed to giving orders, either." Cord came up behind her. The lights of the city were gorgeous from this elevation, sparkling like a million varicolored stars.

"That's hard to believe when you do it so well."

"Abbie, all I want is a legal hold on my baby. If we can accomplish that in any other way...?"

"There is no other way." Abbie turned. "The basis of my decision is time. I cannot sign a paper giving you equal custody when I barely know you." She saw Cord's expression tauten. "If I wasn't worried about my job, I'd suggest we merely see one another until the baby's birth. I've wondered if I'm worrying unnecessarily. Bob Sidwell, the manager of KSTV, is not without compassion, but he's not the final say in important decisions. The station is an independent and there are owners to contend with."

Her eyes narrowed. "But you know all that, don't you? It's what you've been banking on, the reason you've been able to manipulate me so easily."

"Not easily, Abbie. None of this has been easy."

It struck Abbie that he was standing much too close. The slider was at her back. She could smell that marvelous scent he wore and see distinctly that the pupils of his vivid blue eyes contained minute flecks of black. The knit of his sweater seemed to flow over his wide shoulders and muscular upper arms, and the way his jeans fit should be outlawed.

He remembered their night together and she didn't. The inequity of their knowledge was staggering.

"Think about this, Abbie," he said softly. "It's as important for me to know the mother of our child as it is for you to know the child's father. If we try, both of us, our months together could turn out to be a pleasant experience.''

Abbie's throat felt suddenly constricted. For the briefest of moments she wanted to touch him, just stretch out a hand and lay it on his arm. To connect, physically, with the father of her baby. Not in a romantic sense, God forbid, but simply because they were two human beings sharing an experience that truly was a miracle.

Instead, she shaped a rocky, somewhat wavering smile. ''Let's settle the details. It's getting late.''

Cord drew in a disappointed breath. For a second there he'd felt something warm and real from Abbie. ''Whatever you say.'' On the way back to their chairs he asked, ''Are you sure you wouldn't like something to drink? There's orange juice in the refrigerator.'' He managed a smile as she sat down. ''Aren't mothers-to-be supposed to get a lot of vitamin C?''

''Lots of all kinds of vitamins,'' Abbie replied dryly. ''But no, I really don't want anything.''

The sofa received Cord's weight again. ''What does your doctor say about your health?''

''My health is fine.''

''But you were sick at the studio.''

''A little nausea. Nothing to worry about. Cord, please, let's finish up.''

He nodded. ''I called my brother and he's free to fly out here this weekend. I only have to call him back to confirm.''

Abbie's stomach dropped clear to her knees. ''*This* weekend? You're talking about the day after tomorrow?''

''The sooner the better, don't you agree?'' Cord leaned forward. ''Abbie, I'm thinking of you now. You're not showing yet. At least I don't see it if you are.''

His gaze glided down her body to rest, Abbie felt, in the vicinity of her lap. It was an intimate look, the sort of look a man might give a woman who was carrying his child.

The thought was preposterous. Of course she was carrying his child! Why else would she be sitting in his living room on the verge of tears?

"Not this weekend," she said huskily, looking down at her own hands. "Please ... not this weekend."

"But Gary can't get away the following weekend. Abbie. It'll be all right. I know you're busy and upset. I'll take care of everything. You won't have to do anything but go with me to get the license and show up for the ceremony."

Her heart felt as of it were breaking into tiny, irreparable pieces. Meanness, or disregard for her wishes, was much easier to deal with than kindness from him. He wasn't kind, he wasn't! This was merely another tactic he used to have everything go his way!

Abbie's eyes lifted. "You're calling all the shots, apparently."

"You won't let yourself like me, will you? What happened that morning, Abbie? Why did you run off the way you did?"

Picking up her purse from where she had placed it on the floor next to her chair, Abbie got to her feet. "Let me know in the morning when you want to get the license. I'll take my jacket now, please."

Cord rose, slowly. "You're one cool customer, aren't you?"

"Cool? If I said what I was thinking, the paint in this room would blister. My jacket, please?"

Keeping his temper was a test of Cord's willpower during the short trip to the foyer closet. Abbie would try the patience of a saint. Marriage might not be the ideal solution to their dilemma for her, but it wasn't Cord's idea of the best possible usage of the next nine or ten months, either.

But he'd played, there was going to be a baby, and he wasn't going to disappear into the sunset, no matter what Abbie thought of his methods. He wasn't so almighty thrilled with hers, either. He was a heck of a lot more resilient and reasonable than she was, that much was certain.

Cord brought her jacket and offered to hold it for her to put on. Abbie looked him in the eye and took it out of his hands.

Swallowing the buildup of anger in his throat, Cord said tersely, "I'll see you down."

"No, thank you."

"I said, *I'll see you down!*"

Abbie turned away. A fight now wouldn't be funny, not with her mood. Cord's mood, also, seemed stretched to the exploding point. It was better to end this session quickly.

She headed for the foyer. He walked faster and beat her to the door, which he held open. She stalked through it. He followed. Neither looked at the other during the trip to the elevator. Neither said a word during the ride to the first floor.

The elevator doors slid back. "I'll call in the morning," Cord said.

"Fine."

"Where did you park?"

"On the street."

"Then I'll see you to your car."

She didn't argue. What good would it do? Cord Durant did exactly as he pleased!

Stubborn damned woman, Cord thought irately as they left the building and walked to her car. How in hell could the woman he met at that Christmas party and this one be walking around in the same luscious body? That Abbie had been sweet and sexy and funny; this one could make icicles form in a bonfire.

"Good night," he said just as her door slammed shut.

He got nothing in response except for a dirty look.

Sherry's lights were out when Abbie got home. Wearily she went into the house and straight to her bedroom. Her nighttime ritual was rarely ignored, and automatically she removed her makeup, showered and brushed her teeth.

Then, lying in her own bed in the comfort of her own room, she waited for the tears that had threatened her composure at Durant's condominium.

Nothing happened.

Abbie flopped onto her back, her eyes wide and dry. Why wasn't she crying? She was to be married the day after tomorrow to a man she didn't even like, let alone love, so why wasn't she crying? Why, instead of grief, was there a tiny seedling of...

Good Lord, she wasn't looking forward to...?

She couldn't be glad, could she?

No, of course she wasn't glad. How absurd! Only a masochist would be glad about a forced marriage.

*You could leave Vegas. Or face motherhood alone. Tough it out. Say to heck with what anyone might think and march right in to Bob's office in the morning with the biggest news bulletin of the day.*

It felt great to fantasize for a few minutes, but then reality set in again. Abbie sighed. Anchorwomen jobs weren't hanging from the rafters, not in *any* part of the country. Any woman who had secured one had paid her dues, bet on it.

And maybe she was a little cowardly in the bargain. Was it cowardly not to want to start over?

Besides, Durant wasn't so bad. Didn't she usually admire spunk and determination? Apparently she had found plenty to admire in the man last December, Abbie thought wryly, then grimaced. If only she could remember the main event. Cord's comments about it were frustrating. Obviously *he'd* enjoyed the night immensely.

That theory about him possibly wanting money from her was utterly ludicrous. His condo was worth at least three times the value of her house, his furniture as well. And look how quickly he'd snapped up that financial prenuptial condition of hers. The man had assets, make no mistake.

It was odd that he'd insisted on more than a city-hall ceremony, though, regardless of the logic of his arguments. Almost as if he thought theirs was going to be a real marriage.

"Fat chance," Abbie murmured around a yawn. She would sleep in this bed and if Cord stayed here he would use the guest room. End of subject.

As for that mysterious "seedling" she'd noticed, it was probably only gas.

In the morning Abbie wondered if she hadn't misinterpreted some of the conversation at Cord's condo.

But he called before she left the house. "What time are you free today to get the license?"

His voice was becoming familiar, but was that any reason for giddiness? Abbie tossed her head, ridding herself of any such nonsense. "I could take a long lunch break."

"Eleven? Twelve? Give me a time and I'll pick you up at the station."

Panic struck Abbie without warning. It was really happening. They were going to get a license today and be married tomorrow. My God, no one knew! There were hordes of people to tell, some of whom should be invited to the wedding.

"I should have asked last night. Um...you said you were going to handle everything, but do you know where...I mean, is anything planned yet?" Abbie stammered.

"Have you heard of the Winston House?"

"Yes." The Winston House was a marvelous old home that was rented out for parties, usually family-oriented occasions, anniversaries, birthdays and...weddings. Abbie sat down.

"Jack Winston's an old friend. I called him last night after you left. We can have the place between two and four tomorrow afternoon. I've got a caterer lined up and a florist. My brother's plane gets in at eleven in the morning."

"Good Lord," Abbie whispered.

"I talked to a minister, but I've been worried ever since. What's your religious affiliation?"

"A minister's fine," Abbie managed weakly.

"I expect about twenty guests. Will you be inviting anyone?"

"Uh...yes. Yes, of course. Only about five...or ten...I think."

"I ordered mostly white flowers, with a few pastels thrown in. Hope that's all right."

"It's...fine." Abbie's heart had started pumping hard enough to hear. White and pastel flowers? What, in heaven's name, was she going to wear?

"Do you have someone in mind to be your attendant?" Cord asked.

"Uh...yes." Sherry, of course, if she weren't already tied up.

"Good. So, Abbie, what time should I pick you up?"

"Eleven," she said in a faint, reedy voice.

"Are you all right?"

"I'm...in shock."

Cord chuckled softly. "You didn't think I could do it, did you?"

"I'd be the last one to think you couldn't do anything you set your mind to," Abbie said on a deep breath, then wished she hadn't when the tone of Cord's voice changed.

"I'll never get a swelled head around you, will I, Abbie?"

"Nor will I around you," she replied, simply because she had no other response.

"That remains to be seen. I'll see you at eleven. Oh! Do you want me to come in or wait in the car?"

"You might as well come in." Abbie sighed, thinking at the same time that she had news to report to the gang at the station, whether she wanted to or not. There were going to be some mighty surprised faces when she introduced a fiancé today and announced a wedding scheduled for tomorrow.

The minute Abbie put the phone down she ran outside and over to Sherry's house, knocking frantically. Sherry opened the door carrying her purse.

"Oh, hi, Abbie. I'm about to leave for work."

"I know. So am I. Sherry, I...me and Cord Durant...we're getting married tomorrow at two o'clock at the Winston House. Will you be my attendant?"

Sherry smiled. "You know I will."

Abbie's smile was rather shaky. "Thanks. I'll run now."

She was halfway down Sherry's front steps when she heard, "Abbie, what are you wearing?"

Abbie threw up her hands and wailed, "I have no idea."

"Call me later and let me know so I can try to coordinate, okay?"

"Okay. Talk to you later."

Running back into her own house, Abbie stuffed some cosmetics in her purse of the day, sailed to the kitchen and grabbed an orange, then hurried to the garage for her car. She had a million things to do today, which was normal, but

she had to get them out of the way so she could take a long
lunch break.

And if she could find the time, a trip to the Fashion Show
Mall would relieve her mind enormously. Her closet bulged
with good clothes, but in all of those attractive on-camera
outfits, there wasn't one dress suitable for a wedding.

The day moved along at a hectic pace. Abbie endured the
surprised faces before Cord showed up, preferring to spread
the news by herself. When he strolled in at eleven, her knees
got wobbly. Everyone wanted to shake his hand and offer
congratulations, even Ron Harrison. Although Abbie
couldn't help thinking that Ron probably hoped that marriage would lead to retirement for her.

Regardless, Cord was too good-looking in gray slacks and
shirt and a navy blue jacket that had to have been custom
made. Abbie noticed his expensive-looking shoes, the elegant gold watch on his left wrist, the confident set of his
wide shoulders.

He kissed her, a mere brushing of his lips against her
cheek. It took a second to catch on to the snow job he was
giving her friends; the man was an exceptionally good ac-
tor. Abbie's senses reeled in rhythm with her shaky legs.

She concentrated on smiling, doing so until her mouth felt
stretched.

She stopped smiling when they were in his car and heading for downtown Vegas, putting her head back, closing her
eyes.

Cord sent her a glance and returned his gaze to the busy
street. "It went well, don't you think?"

"You didn't have to kiss me."

"We're supposed to be in love," Cord pointed out dryly.
"Lovers kiss. What did you want me to do, shake your
hand?"

Abbie lifted her head. "Stop manipulating me, Cord.
You've got what you wanted. You've won, but the manipulation stops here."

"Fine. The next time we're with friends I'll slap you on
the back like you're one of the guys."

"Oh, don't be ridiculous!"

"Why should one little kiss offend you?"

"Everything about you offends me!" Abbie saw his features tense. Her own jagged nerves were making her say things she didn't mean. "I... I'm sorry. Let's just keep this as nonphysical as possible."

"We need to talk," Cord said after a few minutes. "Will you have dinner with me tonight?"

"I can't. My entire day is planned. Besides, everything's already been said."

"Dammit, Abbie, nothing's been said. You accuse me of manipulation, but that seems to be the only way to get through to you. Can't you put your resentment aside long enough for a little normal conversation? Don't you have questions about me? You said you wanted to get to know me. Pretending I don't exist isn't going to do it."

"Believe me," she said wearily. "I have no doubt about your existence."

The tone of her voice concerned Cord. "Do you feel all right?"

Abbie drew an exasperated breath. "Stop worrying about how I'm feeling. I'm healthy, your baby is healthy."

"A baby is a miracle, Abbie," he said quietly. "Don't resent it."

Her head jerked around to glare at him. "Let's get one thing straight, Cord. I resent you, not the baby. And maybe I wouldn't resent you so much if you weren't running over me like some kind of overly righteous steamroller."

"You'd prefer that I ducked responsibility?"

"I'd prefer..." she started to yell, then halted the flow of anger. "Oh, just drop it, will you? I'm tired of arguing."

"Just keep one thing in mind," Cord said coldly. "I'm no more thrilled about this marriage than you are." At the moment it was the unvarnished truth. Abbie wasn't going to give an inch, and the thought of living with a shrew for nearly a year was damned disheartening.

Abbie turned her face to the side window and furtively wiped away a tear. It was frustrating to be so defenseless. She should probably appreciate Cord's efforts instead of resenting everything he did, but she did feel as if a steamroller were running over her. He was a take-charge man, and never in her life had she been so painfully exposed to one.

It hurt to remember the giddy happiness she and Nick had felt the day they'd gone to get their marriage license. That's how a couple should feel, as if they were walking on air. She felt bogged down today, and from what Cord had just said, so did he.

Their methods might be different, but they were both doing this for their baby. That was the one thought she should try to hang on to. Part of her brain didn't like the way she was behaving, but the other part despised Cord Durant's tactics. Abbie's emotions went in a dozen different directions. She'd like to apologize for her bitchiness and mean it, but an apology would only make her feel better temporarily.

What she wanted desperately to keep from Cord was her choked, hot-eyed urge to cry. He'd probably offer solace, damn him, and if she ever cried on his shoulder she'd despise herself for the rest of her days.

The last few miles to the downtown area were accomplished in strained silence. They became very polite then, with Cord coming around the car to open Abbie's door, and her waiting until he'd done so before getting out. They walked to the courthouse, located the appropriate department, waited in line for about ten minutes and filled out a form. Cord stuck their license in his inside coat pocket. Their eyes met and Abbie looked away first.

They returned to the car. "Got time for lunch?" Cord asked.

"No, I don't." Abbie intended to order something delivered to the station. Planning a long lunch hour hadn't been necessary; she was going to get back well within the limits of her normal break.

They were nearly at the station when Cord asked, "Shall I pick you up tomorrow?"

"My next-door neighbor is going to be my attendant. I can ride with Sherry."

It seemed utterly ludicrous to Cord that he didn't even know Abbie's home address. They had decisions to make, such as when he should take his things to her house.

"Does Sherry know what's going on?" he questioned.

"She's my best friend. I told her everything."

Cord pulled into the station's parking lot and stopped at the front door. "I guess this is goodbye until tomorrow."

"Yes." Abbie reached for the door handle.

"Someone's coming out of the building. That's Ron Harrison, isn't it?"

Abbie glanced over her shoulder and saw Ron giving the car a thorough inspection.

"Better kiss me goodbye," Cord said softly.

"We'll just wait until he passes by."

Gritting his teeth Cord slid across the seat. His arms went around Abbie and he yanked her up against him. "Relax. This won't kill you." Ignoring the panicked look in her eyes, he brought his mouth down on hers. There was more anger than affection in the kiss, but Abbie knew that from Ron's vantage point, the clinch probably looked genuine.

Her own quickened heartbeat startled Abbie. Cord was an overwhelming man. His scent was dizzying and he knew how to kiss. His mouth moved on her wooden lips, urging response, and she wondered why he would kiss her in such a fashion. If this was playacting, he was even better at it than she'd thought. Her insides were turning to mush, scaring the hell out of her. Was this what had happened that night in December? A few kisses of this nature and any woman might lose control!

He raised his head and looked at her. "That wasn't so bad, was it?"

Her heart was beating a mile a minute, and from the heat in her face she knew her cheeks had to be flushed. Confusion racked her when she realized she'd like nothing better than to stay curled up in his arms for the rest of the day. Her only defense to something she didn't understand was anger, which she expressed in a huskily stated, "How dare you kiss me like that? Take your hands off me."

Cord glanced around casually, although there was a ragged catch in his voice. "Sure, no problem. Harrison's gone now." He moved back behind the wheel. "See you tomorrow."

Abbie got out on trembling legs. That shocking kiss demanded something from her, but what? Holding the door open, she mustered a glare. "I've got half a notion to cancel the whole bloody thing!" She slammed the door so hard, the impact rocked the car.

Cord licked his lips, tasting her on them, and watched her storm through the building's front door. He thought about last December and a slow, smoldering smile built on his face. This marriage might not be made in heaven, but it sure as hell wasn't going to be boring.

# Five

---

Abbie bought a new dress. She called Sherry at the bank that afternoon, the result of which was dinner together at the mall after Abbie's broadcast, and some shopping. She didn't feel guilty about evading Cord's dinner invitation, not after that completely unnecessary show of affection in his car. He could have kissed her without so much passion, damn him. The remnants of that kiss had given her hot flashes all afternoon.

Sherry bought a new dress, as well. Abbie's was a dusty pink silk with white trim and Sherry's was in spring shades of blue. They also found Abbie a matching hat with the most cunning rose-tinted veil. On the way to the escalator, Sherry drifted into the store's lingerie department.

"Oh, Ab, look at this," she said wistfully, holding up a gorgeous pink satin teddy.

Abbie looked, admired, pictured herself wearing it for Cord, flushed hotly and finally shook her head. "I don't need it."

Sherry sighed. "Guess not." She put the teddy back on the rack.

As each woman had her own car at the mall, they drove home alone. But they had talked during dinner and Abbie could tell from Sherry's comments that her friend held some hope for the future of this marriage.

Any such hope was inane, Abbie knew, but she herself couldn't deny a strange inner excitement, probably because of that damned kiss. Resentment of Cord's tactics seemed embedded in her system, and yet how many other men would have been as determined to gain legal rights to an unborn child? And Cord had never once questioned his paternity, nor hinted that her morality might be less than lily-white.

Her almost puritan morality made this whole muddle ironic. Other than Cord Durant she had slept with one man, whom she'd married.

At home Abbie hung the new dress in the bedroom closet. It had a few wrinkles, which she would press out in the morning. Getting ready for the ceremony wouldn't take any longer than preparing for any other day.

Frowning slightly, Abbie left her room and went to the guest room, which was across the hall. She switched on the overhead light. Would Cord really use this room? It was entirely possible to visualize him living at his condo, and yet he'd indicated otherwise. How unnerving to have him in the house at all, let alone living here.

Abbie's gaze slowly swept the plain white walls and simple blue bedspread and drapes. The furniture was cherry wood and a good quality. The bed was a queen and should be ample for Cord's height. A nightstand contained a reading lamp, a telephone and a small clock radio. When Nick had become very ill Abbie had slept in here, and the bed was comfortable. But the second bathroom was down the hall and the closet was of a modest size.

It was the only room in the house that would do for a nursery. The third bedroom had been turned into a combination den, library and TV room when she and Nick bought the place. Abbie liked her house and the neighborhood, and she'd never once considered moving after Nick's death.

But it couldn't compare to Cord's lavish condo, not in space, not in decor. It'll be interesting, Abbie mused, to see his reaction to her home.

Instantly her chin came up in a gesture of defiance. Whatever Cord thought of it, this was where she was staying during their farce of a marriage. He could stay or not, that was up to him.

But if he didn't stay, how would she ever learn what kind of person he was?

Snapping off the light abruptly, Abbie closed the door of the guest room. Too jittery to go to bed, she wandered through the house, stopping at the living-room sofa to straighten a pillow, halting again at a painting on the wall to align it more squarely.

Her glance fell on a table laden with framed pictures, most of which were of Nick and her. Biting her lip, Abbie stepped closer to the array. Nick's personal things had long been disposed of, but she had seen no good reason to eradicate every trace of her husband and had left the pictures where they'd always been.

She stood there silently for several minutes, then with no change of expression began to gather up the photographs. Abbie stacked them, one on another, leaving only the one of her parents on the table. She took the stack to the hall linen closet and put them on the top shelf, realizing that it would be very easy to get maudlin and teary right now. If she let herself, she could spend the entire night worrying about how disappointed Nick would be in her, if he were still alive.

It wasn't any way to spend *any* night, and she'd done her grieving, beginning, for that matter, on the day they'd been told how ill Nick really was.

Abbie walked the floor until nearly midnight, then she forced herself to go to bed.

At ten the next morning Sherry called. "Are you getting ready?"

"I'm pressing my dress."

"Are you all right?"

"As all right as I can be, I suppose."

"Need me to do anything for you?"

"No, thanks, Sherry. Everything's under control."

At ten forty-five Cord called. "I'm at the airport to pick up my brother. His plane's going to be about ten minutes late. How's everything on your end?"

"Fine," Abbie replied coolly.

"Abbie, I've been thinking. We should go somewhere for the rest of the weekend. How about my place in L.A.?"

"Why should we go somewhere?"

"It just seems best to give everyone the idea that we're happy about getting married. Most couples go off by themselves after the ceremony, don't they?"

Abbie sucked in a nervous breath. "Why are you doing this?"

"Doing what?"

"Constantly putting me on the hot seat."

Cord's voice cooled. "Look, if you don't give a damn what your friends think, that's fine with me. But I'd just as soon not have *my* friends and *my* brother think that I'd suddenly slipped a cog."

"Maybe you have."

"Dammit, Abbie, this pretense is as much for your sake as mine. More, in fact. I could tell my friends the truth and they'd still be my friends."

"My friends would still be my friends, too," Abbie said angrily. "It's not my friends I'm worried about, which you damn well know."

"If you're so worried about your career, why do you scoff at every suggestion I make? Who did you invite to the wedding?"

"Everyone at the station," Abbie said wearily. "They all can't make it, but there'll be quite a few of my co-workers there. All right, you win...again. If you want to give everyone the impression that we're eagerly dashing off on a short honeymoon, go ahead and do it. But I'm coming home after the ceremony. Whatever you do is your business."

"I can't believe that your never-ending bad humor is good for the baby," Cord said harshly, and broke the connection.

Abbie stared at the dead instrument in her hand. Her never-ending bad humor? "You jerk," she yelled and slammed the phone down.

But Cord's opinion stayed with her while she bathed and dressed. Her mood was definitely nothing to be proud of these days. Whose fault was this mess, anyway? Had anyone forced her to go home with Cord last December? She could blame him, and she did, for burdening her with today's upcoming charade. But shouldn't she also be thanking him? He was saving her butt, to put it bluntly. Instead of an embarrassing explanation to Bob Sidwell, she could smile and blush like any new bride, and then in a reasonable length of time she could announce her pregnancy. A few people might count the months at the baby's birth, but with a wedding ring on her finger no one would do more than whisper about it.

Children outside marriage were no big deal to many people, but regardless of lax morals in some circles, Abbie felt certain that her having a baby without a husband would bring down the roof. At least Cord's determination was going to eliminate trouble from her employers.

Trouble from Cord was becoming customary. He was not a man to be led around by the nose, obviously, and any woman who really fell in love with him would be in for one heck of a roller-coaster ride.

Thank God it wasn't her.

"You look fabulous," Sherry told Abbie during the drive to the Winston House.

"Thanks, but how I look really doesn't matter." If primping for an hour had polished up Abbie's exterior, it had done very little for her inner turmoil.

"It does matter, Abbie," Sherry said quietly. "It's your nature to put your best foot forward, whatever the circumstances."

Abbie couldn't deny Sherry's remarks, even though it would serve Cord right if his befuddled bride showed up for the wedding wearing burlap on her back and curlers in her hair.

Still, there was always a modicum of comfort in knowing one looked one's best. The new pink-and-white dress was a dream, and the tiny veiled hat gave the outfit clarity and a touch of formality. What's more, she could pull the veil down over her eyes, which she was considering doing. Wouldn't her tension be just a tad less noticeable through a rose-tinted veil?

Cars were already lined up at the lovely old house when they arrived. Abbie spotted Cord's and her heart began pounding at the finality of what she was about to do. Marriage was not a game. How could she share her life, her home, her *child* with a stranger? There were intimacies in marriage that had nothing to do with the bedroom. Did she want to know Cord Durant's personal habits? Did she care if he preferred showering at night or in the morning? Which section of the newspaper he read first?

She wasn't sure she liked to cook anymore, and she wasn't going to be responsible for his meals or his laundry. It was probably remiss of her not to have pointed out that Cord wasn't getting himself a maid, a cook or a laundress in their bizarre bargain.

Abbie suddenly felt like bawling. The sun was shining, she was dressed for a wedding and her intended waited inside, and all she could think of was keeping him in his place. Of *putting* him there herself and then making sure he understood how bitterly she viewed their arrangement.

Cord must have been watching for her, she realized when she saw him coming out the front door. He was wearing a pearl-gray suit, which for certain hadn't come off the rack.

"Is that him?" Sherry asked.

"Yes."

"He's an absolute hunk!"

"He's a jerk," Abbie retorted.

Cord smiled as he approached the car. "Lord, Abbie," Sherry whispered. "He's not just handsome, he's gorgeous. Get your head on straight, girl. You're not marrying some common Joe here."

Abbie sent her friend a sharp look, but there wasn't time for further rebuttal. Her car door swung open and Cord peered in.

"Hello, Abbie."

"Hello. Sherry Newman, Cord Durant."

Sherry smiled around Abbie. "Nice meeting you, Cord."

"Nice meeting you, Sherry. Here, let me help you out, Abbie." Cord offered his hand.

Abbie took it with a short "Thanks," and she let go the second she was out of the car. Sherry got out her side and the three of them congregated at the front of the vehicle.

"You look wonderful, Abbie," Cord said softly.

Instead of answering, Abbie slipped the veil down over her eyes. A flush crept up Cord's neck, and both Sherry and Abbie saw the tightening of his mouth.

But he only said, "Shall we go in?" The house had a wide front porch. At the main entrance Cord said, "Sherry, would you mind going in without us? There's something I need to discuss with Abbie."

"I wouldn't mind at all," Sherry replied. She squeezed Abbie's hand. "See you inside, pal."

Abbie managed a weak smile, which got weaker when she and Cord were alone on the porch. "What is it?"

Cord reached into his inside coat pocket and brought out a fold of papers. "Our prenuptial agreement. It's brief and to the point, covering only what we agreed upon. It'll take a minute for you to read and sign it, which I've already done, but it should be completed before the ceremony."

"You're certainly efficient," she drawled, and took the papers and shook out their creases. She read quickly and saw nothing that hadn't been discussed and agreed upon. "Shouldn't this be notarized?"

"A notary is our option. The agreement is fine with me the way it is, but if you want our signatures notarized..."

"No, it's fine. Got a pen?"

"Right here." Cord produced a pen and put it in her hand. "Abbie, there are about forty people inside, and none of them, other than Sherry, knows what's really going on."

Abbie finished signing the document, though she completed her name with short, tight strokes rather than her normal flourish. "You didn't tell your brother?"

"No, I didn't."

"You mean that your own brother thinks this is a real wedding?" Abbie's voice was strident with disbelief.

Cord took the document and tucked it back into his coat pocket. "It *is* a real wedding. Anytime two people stand before a minister and swear to love, honor and whatever else they say nowadays, it's real, Abbie."

"It's hypocritical! You should have told your brother. Now he's going to expect ..."

"Yes, Gary's going to expect you and I to act like any other newly married couple. But so are all the other guests. I saw no point in explaining something to Gary that would only hurt him."

Abbie let Cord's attitude fester for a moment. "You won't hurt your brother, but you're not in the least concerned about hurting me."

Cord took hold of her arm. "I'm not hurting you, dammit, and I'm beginning to think you're not a very nice person! Now, let's go in and get this over with."

*She* wasn't nice? Abbie's lips pursed. "Getting it over with is the first good idea I've heard come out of your mouth," she snapped.

Inside, Abbie saw that everyone was seated. She was glad for the lowered veil, because she was worried about shedding tears before this was over. A tall man in a dark suit stood at the altar with Sherry, obviously Cord's brother. The minister, too, was in place. Soft, lovely background music filtered from unseen speakers. A few people in the audience waved and smiled, and Abbie nodded in acknowledgment.

"Guess everything is ready," Cord muttered at a signal from the minister, and took Abbie's right hand and wrapped it around his arm. "Try to look as though you're not on your way to your own execution."

Abbie pasted on a smile as they began the walk down the aisle, managing in an undertone, "It feels like an execution, although I would rather imagine it being yours than mine."

"If that thought makes you pink-cheeked with elation, dwell on it."

"Oh, I will, make no mistake," Abbie whispered while barely moving her lips. Holding onto Cord's arm was distracting. His remarkably proportioned bulk at her side was distracting. Her skirt brushed against the leg of his trousers as they moved, a disturbing meshing of textures that seemed to reverberate throughout Abbie's entire system.

It was such a miserable farce—the lovely surroundings, the solemnly smiling minister, the expectant faces of friends—that Abbie considered bolting back down the aisle and flinging herself through the ornate front door, leaving everyone to gape and gasp.

But what would she do for an encore, pay a call on Bob Sidwell and confess her sins?

There was a step up onto the platform with the altar, which Abbie didn't notice until she stumbled. Cord steadied her with a murmured, "Careful, darling."

Her eyes widened with shock and her system went into a stall. The minister began speaking, but his words ran together for her. "Wearegatheredheretodayfor..." She shivered and barely registered Cord inching a little closer to her. Her hands and feet felt icy, as if they'd become disconnected from the rest of her body. The minister had a pink glow, everything did, distorted by the veil. She tried to concentrate and heard, "...in the sight of God..." and her lips parted to take in air.

Cord had a death grip on Abbie's elbow. He honestly hadn't expected her to be so shaken. The veil obscured her eyes, but there was an unnatural pallor around her mouth. He thought of her condition and wondered if pregnant women fainted easily.

"Do you, Cord Durant, take Abigail Forbes...?"

"I do."

"Do you, Abigail Forbes, take Cord Durant...?"

Cord waited. The minister waited. The entire assembly waited. Cord leaned his head closer to Abbie's. "Say 'I do,' Abbie."

She dampened her lips and whispered, "I do."

The rings came next, and Abbie was further shaken to see one for Cord in the minister's hand. In very few minutes it

was over. "I now pronounce you man and wife. Mr. and
Mrs. Durant, you may seal your vows with a kiss."

In a daze, Abbie felt a solid kiss being planted on her lips.
And then people began crowding around. She was kissed
and hugged and passed from one set of arms to another till
she was dizzy. Friends and complete strangers blurred one
into the other. Her mouth ached from the strain of so much
smiling.

A strangely familiar arm came around her. "Abbie, I'd
like you to meet my brother. Gary, say hello to my wife."

He looked like an older version of Cord. Maybe not quite
as good-looking, a little more rugged around the edges, but
big and well built and with a smile as large as all outdoors.

"Abbie, sweetheart, I always wanted a sister. Welcome to
the family."

She was hugged so hard she nearly groaned out loud.
From the confines of brawny, masculine arms she watched
Cord's face light up with a silly grin.

"I've been asked to mention refreshments being served in
the next room," the minister announced to the group at
large. "Will the wedding party step over here for signatures
before joining the guests?"

Gary, Cord, Sherry and Abbie followed the minister to a
table while the guests began filing out. Abbie signed her
name where she was told and stepped back. Cord signed
next and moved to stand beside her. His hand slid around
her waist, and when she stiffened, he whispered, "Easy."

Abbie never knew how she got through the next hour.
Two photographers were taking pictures and she vaguely
recalled the glare of flashbulbs during the ceremony. Gary
talked her ear off for at least ten minutes of the brief reception, obviously flying high because of the happy occasion,
and she marveled that his own euphoria at his brother's
good fortune obliterated the impact of her feeble responses. Cord circulated some and was quite the charming
host, but Abbie barely moved from one spot. People kept
coming to her, remarking what a beautiful bride she was,
wishing her the very best, thanking her for the invitation to
her wedding.

And asking her where she and Cord were going for their honeymoon. The first time she was caught off guard and stumbled through a stammered noncommittal reply. After that she merely smiled and said that Cord was keeping their destination a secret, even from her. The romance of a mystery honeymoon seemed to delight everyone and got Abbie off the hook.

Sherry appeared. "You need some lipstick, Ab. Come to the powder room with me."

Relief flooded Abbie's benumbed system. "Yes, thanks."

They wound through the guests and secreted themselves in the powder room. Sherry stood with her back to the door as though guarding it. "Are you as unnerved as you look?"

Abbie sank down on an upholstered bench. "Worse, but I didn't think it showed that much."

"It probably doesn't to anyone else. But I know you pretty well, pal."

Abbie lifted her veil and massaged her temples. "This is the most unholy experience of my life. Do you realize that everyone out there is ecstatic for Mr. and Mrs. Durant? If they only knew."

"But they don't, and you have to get hold of yourself. The worst is over. You and Cord can say your goodbyes and..."

"The worst is over?" Abbie interjected incredulously. "Sherry, the worst hasn't even begun."

"He seems to be an unusually nice guy, Abbie."

"An act." Abbie got up and on her unsteady legs teetered to the mirror. "It's all an act, believe me. Cord's true colors aren't very pretty. He's demanding and overbearing and just plain pushy, and if the next year isn't a living hell I'll exchange my career in broadcasting for a job scrubbing floors."

"Well, you know him a lot better than I do, of course, but he makes a terrific first impression," Sherry said.

"Obviously," Abbie agreed dryly, her eyes meeting Sherry's in the mirror.

Sherry's expression became chagrined. "I wasn't thinking of how the two of you met, Abbie, I swear it."

"Maybe not, but you weren't wrong. Cord *does* make a good first impression. I remember that much about that night, at least."

Cord waited near the door of the powder room. Gary stood with him. "You got yourself a jewel, Cord. Abbie's a special lady."

"Very special," Cord quietly agreed.

"I'm going to try and come back to Vegas for a few days, Cord, maybe next month." Gary grinned. "Would I be welcome?"

"Hell, yes," Cord said emphatically. "Anytime, Gary, anytime at all. Just let me know when, okay?"

"I'll call. I'd like to get to know my new sister-in-law." His grin broadened. "Maybe she'd like to get to know your big brother, too, eh?"

"I'm sure she would," Cord said, noticing the powder-room door opening. "Here she comes. Gary, we're going to have to break this up. Jack Winston squeezed us in as a personal favor. This place is booked for months ahead and there's another party due to begin shortly."

"I understand. Besides, I'd be disappointed in you if you weren't anxious to get that pretty lady alone," Gary said with a laugh and a slap to his brother's back.

Abbie received another round of hugs and good wishes as people began leaving. Gary hung back, as did Sherry, and it seemed perfectly natural for the two of them to fall into conversation.

"You must be a good friend of Abbie's," Gary said.

"A very good friend." Sherry smiled. "*And* her next-door neighbor."

"No kidding? Then we'll be seeing each other next month, if I can arrange the time off. I'm planning on coming back for a couple of days. I'll be staying with Cord and Abbie, of course."

Sherry nodded slowly. "How nice. I'm sure Abbie will be delighted."

"I've got to get to know her, Sherry. She's family now."

"Yes, indeed," Sherry murmured.

With everyone else gone, the four of them walked to the door. They stopped on the porch for goodbyes. Cord and

Gary shook hands and then hugged and pounded each other's back. "Damn, it was good of you to come," Cord said huskily. "Did you call a taxi? We can't just leave you standing here."

"Do you need a ride somewhere?" Sherry inquired.

"To the airport," Gary answered. He looked at his watch. "My plane leaves in an hour."

"I'll drop you off," Sherry volunteered.

"That would be great, Sherry," Cord said. "Thanks."

"It's no problem," Sherry said, and turned to Abbie for a hug. She whispered in her ear, "For God's sake, don't hurry home. Go somewhere, if Cord suggests it. Give him a chance, Ab."

And finally, the earthshaking event was truly over. Abbie got into the front seat of Cord's car. Gary and Sherry drove away. Abbie twisted the gold ring on her finger. Cord got behind the wheel and started the engine.

Then he looked at her. "How ya doing?"

She took a long, slow breath. "Okay, I guess."

"You came through like a trooper. I don't think anyone suspected a thing, do you?"

"I have no idea. It all passed in a fog for me."

Cord's glance fell on her left hand. "What do you think of the ring?"

"It's obviously expensive. So is yours. I didn't expect a double-ring ceremony."

"But do you like it?"

"It's a beautiful ring, but..."

"There's always a 'but' with you, Abbie, isn't there?" He paused. "Please raise that veil so I can see your eyes."

She hesitated, resigned herself to scrutiny and brought the veil up.

"Look at me, Abbie," Cord said softly.

Her head turned slowly, and when Cord was looking directly into her eyes something tightened and tensed within her.

"I wondered if I would feel any different," Cord said. "Do you? Feel differently, I mean?"

She felt immeasurably different. The ring on her finger was an unfamiliar weight and constriction. There was life beginning in her womb. Only a few weeks ago her thoughts were almost entirely focused on her job, and now she couldn't seem to focus them on any subject.

Oh, yes, she felt very different. But tell Cord her innermost feelings?

No, she wasn't ready for confidences.

Cord could practically read her mind from the reluctance in her eyes. "Well . . . have you thought any more about going to California? We could be there in time for a late dinner. My house has several extra bedrooms and plenty of space. Getting away together might give us a good start, Abbie."

The thought of any kind of honeymoon raised Abbie's resistance. She glanced out the window as two cars drove into the parking lot; apparently people were beginning to arrive for the next event at the Winston House.

"I'd really rather just go home," she said quietly. "You do whatever you wish, of course. I'd like that aspect of . . . of this relationship to be perfectly clear. Both of us are free to come and go without explanation."

Cord slammed the shifting lever into reverse. "Maybe we should have put that in the agreement."

Abbie turned in the seat. "Why does my attitude make you angry? We have no hold on one another."

Instead of driving off, Cord gave her a hard look. "Maybe something else should have been put in the agreement. As long as we're married, I'll behave accordingly."

Abbie couldn't tear her gaze from his. "You're talking about . . . other women?"

"I'm talking about fidelity."

"That's absurd. As long as you're reasonably discreet . . . I mean, why should you live a celibate life for a year?"

"You will, won't you?"

"Well, of course, but . . ."

"Stop with the 'buts,' Abbie," Cord said wearily and put the car in motion with a light foot pressure on the gas pedal. "I've got some clothes in the trunk. What's your address? We might as well get this show on the road."

# Six

The closer they got to Abbie's neighborhood, the tenser she became. They were married. He had agreed to separate beds, but did she trust him? Getting down to brass tacks, was there any good reason why she *should* trust him?

She drew a shaky breath. Dare she trust herself? Didn't she have immutable proof of the man's charm? "You really are planning to move into my house?" she finally asked.

Cord sent her a questioning glance. "That was our agreement. Do you prefer another arrangement? My condo, maybe?"

"No, no," Abbie said quickly. "It's just that..." She bit her lip. "May I speak frankly?"

"I wish you would."

"Well..." Abbie was frowning and knew it, but the situation was awful enough to be confusing. They were two strangers and married. It made no sense. Putting aside that indistinct night in December, they had never shared a meal, had never carried on any sort of normal conversation and knew virtually nothing about each other except for information of a public nature. Setting up housekeeping to-

gether seemed utterly ludicrous, but behind that opinion for
Abbie was one hard, inescapable fact: without proximity
they would never get beyond this same uncomfortable alli-
ance, and wasn't the reasoning behind this farce based on
discovery?

Abbie suffered a sinking sensation as she admitted again
that Cord's threats to bring her private life public had really been the deciding factor, which wasn't something she
could easily forget. Regardless, refusing the trip to California had probably been a mistake. Cord seemed determined
to prolong this ghastly day, and which was better, or worse:
spending hours in his car together or hours at her house together?

"If that invitation to drive to California is still open, I'd
like to change my mind about accepting," Abbie said.

"Great." Cord sent a pleased smile in her direction. "But
I thought you wanted to speak frankly about something."

Abbie looked down and her gaze caught on the ring on
her left hand. Her head immediately started aching. "Maybe
frankness isn't a good idea." She brought her eyes up
abruptly, unable to look at the ring for long.

"We won't get anywhere without honesty, Abbie."

"I can tell you one thing frankly. Real friendships take
time for me."

Cord nodded. "I can relate to that. We'll let things happen naturally, okay?"

"It would be best," Abbie concurred. "Turn right at the
next corner."

Following Abbie's instructions, Cord maneuvered the car
through a quiet residential area. "Nice neighborhood."

"I like it."

"Lived here long?"

"Three years. That white house on the left is mine."

Cord pulled into the driveway and turned off the engine.
"Do you have just the one car?"

"Only one. Why?"

"Then there's room in your garage for mine."

To her credit, Abbie hesitated only a moment. "I'll give
you the extra remote control for the door. It won't take me
long to change and pack an overnight case."

"Take your time. I've got to haul in my things anyway."

"Come in first and I'll show you your room."

Unexpectedly for Abbie, Cord reached out and touched the veil of her hat. "You look good in a hat, Abbie. Not every woman does, you know."

Abbie's pulse went wild. There was something between them that was better left alone. Compliments and seemingly casual touching were not innocent pastimes for them. Ducking her head, she reached for the door handle. "Let's go in."

She knew he was sizing up everything while she unlocked the front door of the house; the shrubbery, the three mature palm trees and the lawn all got an inspection. The walled backyard contained a pool and yards of cement, artfully decorated with potted plants and patio furniture, but Abbie didn't feel comfortable enough to conduct a tour.

"This way," she said as she started through the house. She stopped at the guest-room door and pushed it open. "This will be your room. The second bathroom is across the hall."

"Uh-huh," Cord acknowledged. "Looks fine to me. I'll go get a load."

"There are hangers in the closet," Abbie reminded as he strode back down the hall. When he was out of sight she slumped against the wall, letting the limpness that had threatened her composure for the past hour and a half take over completely. For a few blessed moments she went totally blank, retreating to a private spot within herself without strife or tension.

But then she heard Cord coming in and she pushed herself away from the wall and hurried into her bedroom, closing the door behind her.

While Abbie changed clothes and packed a small suitcase, she heard Cord making several more trips to his car. His moving in had an unreal quality, and she realized uneasily how clearly sound carried in the house, and that if she could hear him he could hear her.

Her privacy was a thing of the past. Cord would know every time she got up in the night, when she showered and for how long. He would hear her hair dryer, the flushing of

her toilet, her footsteps whenever a restless night made
walking the floor more attractive than rolling and tossing.

They were married. Dear God. Abbie put her hands on
the sink in her bathroom and let her head fall forward. If she
cried now she'd have red eyes, but crying until she passed
out held a perverted appeal.

She pulled herself upright and opened a drawer for her
hairbrush. After using it, she gathered an armful of personal items and brought them to the suitcase on her bed.

And then there were no excuses left for dawdling; she was
as ready for a weekend trip to California with Cord—with
her *husband*—as she ever would be.

It didn't take Cord long to move in. He'd brought most
of his clothes on hangers, which merely required a trip from
the car to his new closet. Underwear, socks and incidentals
were transferred from suitcases to bureau drawers, shoes
were lined up on the closet floor. Any other personal items
he wanted, he'd transfer from his condo little by little.

He checked out the room. It wasn't large but had every
convenience, even a telephone on the bedstand. His as-
signed bathroom was well supplied and spotlessly clean,
which didn't surprise him. After exchanging his suit and
dress shoes for jeans and loafers, he tossed a few things into
his smallest suitcase, added his shaving gear and brought the
case out to the car.

He came in again to wander through Abbie's house. It
had a homey feeling. Her furniture was an eye-catching
mixture of modern and antique, not a combination that
everyone could carry off as well as Abbie had. Her kitchen
was large and contained a round table and four chairs. What
had apparently been intended as a third bedroom had been
turned into a den, and the room contained the only television set in the house, unless Abbie had one in her bedroom.

Cord stood at the French doors in the kitchen-dining area
and studied the backyard. That's where he was when he
heard Abbie. He turned. "I like your house, Abbie."

"Thank you."

Cord's gaze moved over her tan slacks and sweater. Their married state suddenly struck him as meaningful. She looked great in casual clothes, comfortably stylish, and he'd always thought her pretty, even before they had met, when she was only an image on the TV screen. The bottom line was that he liked more than Abbie's house, but he knew that saying so would knock their faltering relationship backward by about twenty paces. "Ready to go?"

She nodded. "My suitcase is in the foyer."

A dozen ideas passed through Cord's mind. He wished he could smooth out the lines on her forehead, relieve the tension crinkles at the corners of her eyes, do something to make her smile, or better yet laugh.

He would like to say, "It won't be so bad, Abbie. You might even end up liking me."

He merely said, "Is everything secure in the house?"

"Unless you unlocked the back door. Did you?"

"No."

But Abbie, accustomed to relying on herself, came around him to try it, which brought her very close. Cord furtively inhaled her scent and experienced a bittersweet awareness in his gut. That night in December leaped to clarity in his mind, and he thought about reminding her of it.

He smiled when she looked at him, stifling every impulse. "Shall we go, then?"

Abbie locked the front door on the way out. Cord carried her suitcase to the car and put it in the trunk with his. Abbie settled herself on the front passenger seat as Cord got behind the wheel and started the engine.

They drove away, each involved in his own thoughts.

When they were on the interstate, Cord said, "I usually fly to California. Haven't driven there in quite a while." After a pause, he asked, "Do you get to L.A. very often?"

"I have no reason to go there."

"How'd you get started in broadcasting, Abbie?"

She sighed. "It's a long, dull story, Cord."

"Tell me about it."

She tried to sound as though she'd left impatience and reluctance in Las Vegas, but completely forgetting Cord's

overbearing tactics in getting things his way wasn't possible
so soon, and her voice remained cool.

"My first media job after college was with a small radio
station. I was little more than a gofer, but I fell in love with
the energy of the place."

Abbie's story encompassed several different employers,
but it was obvious that each of her career moves had
brought her closer to her present position. Cord listened at-
tentively, as much to the tone and nuances of her voice as
her words. She wasn't enjoying talking to him, probably
resented giving him information about herself. There was
unrelenting rigidity in her posture and in the way she kept
her eyes on the road.

He gave an inward sigh. The path to any kind of normal
relationship for them was snarled with heavy-duty hurdles
and in the back of his mind was the question that kept
hounding him: Why would a woman with her stringent
outlook go to bed with a man she had only just met? That
night had to have been a major deviation for Abbie, but he
never could have reached that conclusion from her loose and
lighthearted mood at the time. She'd been like a beautiful
butterfly, flitting, teasing, laughing, making him fall a little
bit in love with her, bedazzling him. The following morning had been like the landing from a long, unexpected fall,
hard and abrupt and shaking the romantic cobwebs from his
system.

Abbie could feel her tension mounting again; the farther
they got from Las Vegas the worse it became. She talked
faster and tried to ignore the sensation, rambling about
people and events that Cord couldn't possibly have any desire to hear.

To cover her own disorganized thoughts, she questioned
him about his career. Willingly, pleased that she would ask,
Cord explained about Gary giving him a camera for his
fourteenth birthday and how quickly he'd taken to photography. What he didn't explain was the instant connection he
had felt with the art form, without even knowing that it was
art he was dabbling in.

The miles clicked by, with Abbie intently watching the
road. The Nevada/California state line seemed like a final

straw. She dampened her lips. "Please...would you pull over?"

Cord gave her a startled look. "Are you ill?"

Her hands rose to her face. "No...yes...just pull over. Please."

Quickly Cord steered onto the wide shoulder and stopped the car, not knowing what to expect. "Abbie...are you all right?"

She lowered her hands. "You're probably going to think I'm slightly deranged, but I don't want to go to California. Would you please turn the car around and take me home?"

He looked at her for the longest time, then said quietly, "I'll take you home, but would you tell me why?"

She couldn't look directly at him. "It just doesn't feel...right."

"What doesn't? Talking to me? Going somewhere with me? Abbie, we're married. We have a right to do anything we want."

Then she did look at him, a slow turning of her head that brought her gaze to his. He *did* expect something from the weekend, and she was afraid to find out what it was. "I can't do this, Cord. I never should have agreed. I want to go home and I want you to move back to your condo."

Cord's features tensed. "It's a little late to change your mind, don't you think?"

Abbie bit her lip, wary of breaking down and doing something totally female, such as bursting into tears. "You pressured me. I didn't have enough time to think it through. Everything's been your way from the moment you found out about the baby."

"So you want us to live separately? Aren't you concerned with what people will think?"

"Right now I don't care what anyone might think. I need some time, the time you refused to give me while you were so determined to force me into choosing one of your options. You're not a fair man, Cord. Have you once put yourself in my shoes? I was pressured from every direction, worried about my job, worried about the baby, worried about what you might do. Well, you got what you wanted, but you can't force me to like it. I do not want to spend the weekend in California with you, nor do I want you living in my house."

Abbie faced front again. "Now please turn the car around and take me home."

"And then what? Are you saying you don't intend to see me again? Abbie, that isn't going to happen. If you try to stop this without giving it a chance, I'll…" Cord halted the flow of angry threats; there'd been enough threats between them. "Abbie, be reasonable. All right, I can see where you might be feeling pushed. But we can work it out. If you're not comfortable with me staying at your house full-time, we'll try it part-time."

"Not tonight," Abbie said with sudden frost in her voice. He had come close to threatening her with his attorney again, damn him.

"Fine, not tonight," Cord agreed tersely. After checking for traffic, he wheeled the car back onto the highway and began watching for an overpass or some way to get headed back to Las Vegas. He wanted to keep this peaceable, but Abbie wasn't making it easy.

"You can cross the median there," Abbie pointed out at the first sign of a flat space between the two highways.

"It's not a legal cut," Cord said brusquely.

"Use it anyway!"

"Fine!" Cord made a sharp left turn and illegally crossed the median. Rocks flew up from the tires and he braked, then sped up to enter the flow of traffic heading into Nevada. In no more than ten seconds a highway-patrol car was behind them, with flashing lights and a wailing siren.

"I hope you're satisfied," Cord hissed.

"Oh, damn," Abbie muttered. "Don't worry, I'll pay the fine."

Fifteen minutes later they were moving again. The fine for illegally crossing the median was a whopping one hundred and fifty dollars.

"Give it to me," Abbie demanded. "I'll send a check."

"You will in a pig's eye," Cord snarled, and stuffed the ticket into his shirt pocket.

They rode in strained silence. "You're behaving like a child," Abbie accused.

"That makes two of us."

"You're only mad because I won't go to California."

"Damned right I'm mad," Cord conceded. "But not because you won't go to California. You're totally unreasonable. How in hell are we supposed to get to know each other if you refuse to try? Abbie, I'm willing to bend over backward to make this work. I'll do anything you suggest within reason, but you've got to try."

Abbie closed her eyes. It galled her to admit it, but he was right. It was just that she didn't know how to behave in such an unholy situation. What woman would? He was too good-looking, and she kept remembering snatches of that night in his condo. Vague as those memories were, the kiss he had forced upon her for Ron Harrison's benefit was crystal clear. At the first opportunity, Cord would take advantage of her weakness for him, which he had to know a lot more about than she did. How *should* she behave under such trying circumstances?

And yet she had agreed to this sham marriage, never mind that her acquiescence had been the result of extreme duress. Wasn't it better to at least try to conform? They were in this for the long haul, and writing it off after only a few hours was undoubtedly hasty.

She sat there for another mile or so without speaking and finally conceded, "All right. You can stay at the house, but there'll be no trips together. And don't expect me to worry about your meals or anything else."

"Anything else, like what?"

"Like laundry."

Cord laughed humorlessly. "Good Lord, have you been worrying about me expecting you to do my laundry? Abbie, I've been taking care of myself for more years than I care to remember. I'm thirty-three years old, for Pete's sake. I've functioned very well without a wife, and believe me, it never once entered my mind that marriage would automatically transfer any personal responsibility from my shoulders to a woman's."

Abbie felt revoltingly foolish. When she married Nick had she told him not to expect meals and clean laundry from her?

But she had loved Nick, and doing things for him had seemed natural and wonderful to her.

She resented Cord, and the thought of any show of sub-servience made her cringe.

As foolish as she felt, she kept her chin up. "Fine. We understand each other."

"Like hell we do," Cord muttered, thinking that this relationship might not ever get off the ground. It seemed utterly impossible that Abbie was picking at such insignificant routines as laundry and meals. He would handle his dirty clothes as he always did, load them up and drop them off at the cleaners. He liked the way they did his shirts anyway. As for meals, if neither of them felt like cooking they could eat out.

They were almost back to Abbie's house when she said, "I really would like to be alone tonight."

"Don't worry, you will be. I've got my overnight bag in the trunk. I'll carry in your suitcase and be on my way."

He'd answered so quickly, Abbie gave him a sharp look. There was no misinterpreting his mood: he was royally ticked.

Oddly, she felt no elation over her victory. This whole miserable affair had her feeling like the car seat was con-structed of needles. As wedding days went, this one had to be an all-time low. Second-guessing her decision to take his third option hurt like hell, because with the horrible fact behind her, it seemed as if she could have found some other solution.

It wasn't until she was in her house and Cord had driven away that she faced reality again. Cord was not going to permanently distance himself from the woman carrying his child. What's more, deep down where it counted she knew that Cord had as much "right" on his side as she did. She might resent his methods, but innate fairness demanded recognition of the soundness of his motives.

As late afternoon faded into evening, Abbie left the lights off and sat in the gathering darkness. The day had been draining, but as night descended she admitted her childish behavior today. There was no room in her life for petulance or pouting. Wanting the best for her baby was what had prompted her to seek out Cord in the first place.

She promised herself to do better at their next meeting, although only the Lord knew when that would be, since Cord had driven off angry.

Abbie wanted to go to church on Sunday morning, but a few of the people who had been at the wedding attended her church and she didn't feel up to dealing with curiosity about why a brand-new wife would go anywhere without her brand-new husband. Besides, too many friends had heard that "mystery honeymoon" story, and ostensibly she was out of town.

She didn't even want to see Sherry, and when Sherry left in her car around ten that morning without glancing at Abbie's house, Abbie knew that her friend hadn't seen Cord drop her off yesterday.

By four in the afternoon Abbie was ready to talk to someone and wished Sherry would return from wherever she'd spent the day. Keeping an eye out for Sherry's car through the window, Abbie saw, instead, Cord's vehicle arriving.

She backed away from the window with her heart fluttering peculiarly. Certainly she hadn't hoped he would come back today, but there was no mistaking the spurt of excitement she felt because he was ambling up her front walk.

She opened the door. "Hello."

"Hello, Abbie. May I come in?"

"Yes, of course." Abbie stepped back.

"Thanks."

Yesterday's tension hadn't abated a whole lot, Abbie thought unhappily as she led the way to the living room. Had he come to stay? Maybe only to test her mood? She'd vowed to do better at their next meeting, but did she have the stomach for pretense when she really felt like bawling?

"Sit down if you like," she invited with a flicking of her hand.

"Thanks. We need to talk, Abbie."

"Probably." She sat in one of her matched wing chairs.

Cord chose the sofa. "I put in a strange night, Abbie. I kept waking up, every hour on the hour. Ever have a night like that?"

"I'm sure everyone has at one time or another."

"You know what I think, Abbie? I think you don't believe in my sincerity."

Her lips twitched in a slightly incredulous reaction. "I really haven't given your sincerity any thought one way or another. But now that you've brought it up, what really do you want me to believe that you're so sincere about?"

"About wanting the baby, of course."

She scoffed openly. "Believe me, I know you want the baby."

Cord leaned forward. "I don't only *want* my baby, Abbie, I want to smooth the way for him. I want his parents to be comfortable with each other. I want you and I to be on good enough terms to discuss any and all problems that might come up. When I drive away with the little tyke, I don't want you worrying, and when he's with you, *I* don't want to worry."

His "driving away with the little tyke" was precisely the sort of nightmare Abbie had been attempting to deal with all along. Her maternal protectiveness was already well-defined, apparently, because the thought of anyone "driving away" with her baby gave her a cold chill.

But...her own preferences were losing acuity. Cord's logic was no different than her own in this instance. She was weary of their going-nowhere battle and seemingly settling into a fatalistic resignation. The hard facts were that the two of them were in this together, not quite joined at the hip until after the baby's birth, but close. It was time to concede to inevitability, to get on with her life, and to do so with as much normalcy as she could manage.

"I agree," she said quietly, her calm demeanor concealing an inner struggle to bury resentment once and for all.

Cord stared. Abbie was the most unreadable person he'd ever known. Every time he looked at her he remembered how excitingly uninhibited she had been that one incredible night in December and then marveled that she appeared *never* to think about it. Take right now, for instance. Wasn't their lovemaking on her mind just a little, even though they were talking about an unmistakably serious subject? How could she help thinking about it, when the substance of their conversation was because of that night?

"You agree to what, Abbie?" he questioned, his voice softened by the direction of his thoughts.

"To... to our original agreement, of course," she stammered, a little disoriented by Cord's intensely admiring inspection. Her face suddenly flamed: he was thinking about that night!

She got up. "I don't usually cook on Sunday, but I made a pot of stew this morning. Would you like to stay for dinner?"

Cord rose from the couch. "Yes, I would. Thanks."

Nothing was said about him staying for the night, but to Cord there seemed to be a tentative understanding in the air. To Abbie's dismay, Cord followed her to the kitchen. She began fluttering from stove to counter to refrigerator, trying to align her frazzled thoughts.

"I'll help," Cord said. "Tell me what you want me to do."

"Help? Uh..." Abbie was at the refrigerator, and it took intense concentration to remember what ingredients went into a green salad. Cord so obviously thinking about that night had flustered her so badly her hands shook as she brought out lettuce, celery and a cucumber. "I guess you could make the salad."

Cord smiled. "I'm a darned good salad maker."

Abbie's smile was weak, but at least she had one. "The bowls are in that cabinet," she indicated with a nod of her head.

Cord opened the cabinet door and studied the array. "Any one in particular?"

"You decide."

It was unnerving to share her kitchen with Cord. Abbie turned on the burner under the stew and went to another cabinet for dishes to set the table.

"The vegetables are clean," she said when Cord reached for the plastic bag of lettuce. "I always wash them before putting them away."

Cord began tearing lettuce into the crystal bowl he'd chosen. "I thought from your house that you're an organized person. Washing salad vegetables before putting them away proves it." *So, how come an extraordinarily organized woman made such a monumental mistake last December?* Damn, he wished he could come right out and ask that question. More accurately, he wished that she could deal with it by answering honestly. For some unimaginable reason she preferred pretending it hadn't happened, which was slightly ludicrous given its result.

But at least she was trying now. Having a meal together was a huge step for them. There was a friendly sort of intimacy in sharing a kitchen, of walking around each other, of Abbie murmuring apologies when she needed to get into the cutlery drawer, which he was blocking, of him saying "Excuse me," and moving to one side.

Abbie wasn't sure she knew up from down at the moment. Cord was bothering her on an unexpectedly personal level. She kept remembering that kiss in his car. Her resentment was buried deep enough, she hoped, that it wouldn't surface and ruin every effort she made in this outlandish arrangement. But his size seemed exaggerated in her kitchen, and more disturbing, his good looks. He wore casual cream-colored cotton slacks and a cream T-shirt that proclaimed in red letters that he was a Rebels' booster. Abbie, too, was a fan of the University of Las Vegas's basketball team, and owned, for that matter, a shirt with the same message, which gave them one common denominator.

But Cord's clothing wasn't the issue, it was how he filled it. Simple cotton slacks on a man shouldn't make a woman want to shriek, but Cord had the greatest behind she'd ever seen. Abbie kept averting her eyes, but his back was to the kitchen at large, and every time he moved her gaze landed on his buns.

It was ridiculous and out of character for her. She didn't stare at men's behinds, nor at their zippers. But while she bustled around the kitchen, attempting to look as if she knew exactly what she was doing when her mind was really only spinning ineffectually, a frightening idea wormed its way into the almost choking convolutions of her thoughts:

only something very powerful could have caused her to leave that Christmas party with Cord . . . to go to his condo with him . . . to make love with him.

Abbie's movements became sluggish with discord: discovering this man's power again would only bring her additional stress. It was something she must guard against, if she managed nothing else.

So . . . how did a woman convey friendliness, when every fiber of her being was telling her to beware?

# Seven

"This stew is really great," Cord said as he helped himself to another ladle from the serving bowl.

Abbie thought the stew was only so-so, but accepted his verdict with a murmured, "Thanks."

Their dinner conversation had touched on the weather, the neighborhood and on Las Vegas politics, accomplished with a good many uneasy starts and unsettling silences.

Abbie got up and brought a plate of sweet biscuits and fresh fruit to the table for dessert, then nibbled on a peach while Cord finished his meal.

He put down his fork and sat back. "It was great, Abbie." She smiled faintly in response. "I'll cook tomorrow night."

"If you wish."

He laughed. "I detect some doubt about my cooking ability. I'm not in your league, but I do pretty well with a barbecue grill. What part of the chicken do you like best?"

Abbie shrugged. "Anything but the thighs."

"I'll barbecue some breasts and legs tomorrow night."

They exchanged gazes across the table. An onlooker would have seen a handsome couple winding up a satisfying meal, but both Cord and Abbie were thinking of how tentative was their progress. "Are you planning to stay here tonight?" Abbie asked quietly.

"I'd like to, but I'll do whatever you want." Cord paused, then added softly, "I'd give a lot to see a genuine smile on your face, Abbie. Making you unhappy was never my intention. I promise you that I will never knowingly or deliberately do anything to cause you pain. Please believe that."

Without warning, something cracked wide open in Abbie, and when it did an overwhelming urge to cry tightened her throat to the point of agony. Unable to speak, she stumbled to her feet.

Alarmed, Cord got up. "Abbie..."

She shook her head and hurried from the kitchen. If she were finally going to break down and bawl, it wasn't going to happen in front of Cord.

But he was so shaken by the frightened-deer look on Abbie's face that he followed, catching up with her at her bedroom door. "Abbie," he said and tried to pull her into his arms. Not for anything sexual, but because she looked so damned forlorn.

"No, don't," she croaked, and pushed against him. But the dam had broken and the tears she had vowed to keep private were flooding her face.

"Abbie, Abbie," Cord pleaded, and held her to his chest until she stopped struggling. While she sobbed he stroked her hair, her back, and she didn't have the strength to fight his kindness. Standing there, up against him, all of the pent-up anger and resentment of recent weeks drained out of Abbie in the form of huge crocodile tears. His T-shirt became soggy, but still he held her and still she wept.

Her sobs gradually gave way to sporadic hiccups. Abbie needed a tissue but didn't want to leave Cord's arms to get one. For the first time in weeks she felt safe, although she was clearheaded enough to wonder why the very man causing her misery would also give her a sense of safety.

Except, strangely, she didn't feel nearly as miserable now as she had before. This crying spell had been brewing for a long time, certainly since her appointment with Dr. Leighton, maybe even before that. Maybe, in all honesty, since December.

Shaping a teary smile, Abbie inched away from the security of Cord's embrace. "I have to blow my nose."

"Want my handkerchief?" Cord offered.

"I'll get a tissue, thank you."

She went through her bedroom and into her bathroom. Ignoring her puffy eyes in the mirror, she blew her nose and washed her face. It seemed unbelievable that the horrible tension she had been living with was gone, but it was true. The situation suddenly seemed bearable, the agreement between her and Cord, and even the pretense with friends she would have to live with until after the baby's birth. Her life was not over because she had gotten herself into a serious jam; Cord was not an ogre, no more than she was an ogress.

The comparison made Abbie smile and she gave herself a really good look in the mirror, astonished that the smile was genuine. She drew in a shaky breath, recalling Cord's comment about wanting to see a genuine smile on her face.

It was time to get on course, to face Cord on a mature equal basis, to accept his point of view about the baby and to meet him halfway in their unusual arrangement.

She should have had this cry days, weeks ago, she thought as she brushed her hair and dabbed on a little lipstick.

Calm and reasonably collected, Abbie left her room. She found Cord clearing the table in the kitchen. He stopped with a plate in his hand. "Are you all right?"

"I'm fine." Abbie moved to a chair, where she laid her hands on the top of its seat back. "I'd like to apologize."

"That's not necess . . ."

"Yes, it is. I'm sorry for being so . . . well, bitchy. I think I went into shock when Dr. Leighton told me I was pregnant and the feeling just kept getting worse until a few minutes ago."

"You've been tense."

"Tense enough to shatter," Abbie agreed. "Anyway, I'm willing to work sensibly on our . . . situation."

Cord stepped to the counter and set the plate down. "I'm glad, Abbie. I'd like us to be friends." His eyes narrowed slightly, because he'd have liked more than friendship with Abbie. She was his wife, and while that might not mean anything to her it was becoming acutely meaningful to him. Her crying in his arms had made him feel extremely protective, even possessive. Maybe his feelings were becoming so pronounced and disturbing because he'd never before had a wife, but he couldn't imagine experiencing the same emotions with any other woman.

"Friends, yes. I'll try," she promised.

He believed her. "Thanks, Abbie. You won't regret it."

"So," Abbie said to Sherry after a sip from her glass of water in Hellerman's Café a month later. "We've been getting along ever since." The two women hadn't really talked before today, as Sherry had been in Reno at one of her bank's branches on a special assignment. On this Tuesday, they were catching up.

Sherry smiled. "I'm very glad, Abbie. I couldn't help wondering."

"But don't look for more than friendship between Cord and me," Abbie cautioned.

"Of course not," Sherry replied.

"You said that much too smoothly," Abbie accused. "Surely you've never hoped for anything permanent out of our arrangement."

"Heavens, no."

"Sherry! Stop looking like a cat with a bowl of cream."

Sherry laughed. "You're too suspicious, Ab. I know your marriage is temporary, but I'll tell you something, pal. If Cord Durant was my husband, he wouldn't get away very easily."

"I wish he were your husband," Abbie retorted.

Sherry's left eyebrow went up. "And that I was having the baby?"

"Well," Abbie said reluctantly. "I guess not." Her expression became soft and introspective. "A baby. I wonder if it's a boy or a girl."

"You can find out, you know."

"Yes, Dr. Leighton explained that. I've been thinking about it."

"What does Cord say?"

"I . . . haven't discussed it with him."

"But you're going to, aren't you?"

Abbie sighed. "I haven't decided."

They ate their chicken salads in silence for a few moments. "Is Cord still gone several nights each week?" Sherry asked.

"He has to spend time at his studio in Los Angeles."

"And how have the two of you been doing on weekends?"

"He . . . catches up at his Vegas studio on weekends, and with . . . personal matters, I guess," Abbie said slowly. "I haven't suggested spending weekends together, Sherry. He stays at his condo." Abbie spoke faster and with more force. "I really have no idea what he does on weekends, but don't misunderstand. Whatever he does is fine with me." She gave a brief laugh. "He has a right to do anything he wants."

"A sensible arrangement," Sherry murmured.

Abbie's eyes dropped to her plate. "Yes, sensible." Why, if it were so sensible, was she beginning to question, privately, of course, what Cord did on weekends? He had tried to mingle their first weekend as man and wife and she had refused. She had been working on a special project for the station during their second weekend together, which had eliminated any such decision. But two more had passed, and Cord had disappeared on Saturday morning and not returned until Sunday night.

They had been married for exactly a month today. It wasn't an anniversary to celebrate, given their awful wedding day, but the date kept gnawing at Abbie and she couldn't help wondering if Cord was aware of it.

"You're looking wonderful," Sherry told her. "Your complexion is fabulous and I don't see a sign of a tummy yet."

Abbie mustered a grin. "I'm expanding, make no mistake, but it's still concealable."

"Have you told anyone at the station?"

"I'm planning to announce it next week. I'd do it yet this week but Bob's on vacation. Are you finished with Reno, Sherry?"

"For a while. I might have to go back in a few months, but we'll see. By the way, have you heard from Cord's brother?"

Abbie dabbed her mouth with her napkin. "I think Cord hears from Gary on a regular basis." Her eyes sparkled teasingly. "Interested?"

"Yes, to be honest," Sherry said. "But that's not why I brought up his name. At the wedding he mentioned coming to Vegas for a few days, expressly to get to know you, and I was merely wondering . . ."

"He said he was coming back? When?"

Sherry thought for a moment. "Seems like he said a month or so."

Abbie was frowning. "Cord mentions Gary every so often, but he didn't say anything about him coming back so soon. I've avoided any at-home entertaining, Sherry—I'm sure you can figure out why—and Gary's presence could put an awful strain on Cord's and my truce."

"Is that how you see your present relationship, Abbie, as a truce?"

Abbie sighed again. "I don't know why I called it a truce. We've been fairly comfortable with each other. When he's in town, he cooks or I do. He's an excellent houseguest, actually. His bathroom and bedroom are always neat and..."

"Houseguest, Abbie? He's your husband."

Abbie's fists clenched and she hid them in her lap beneath the tablecloth. Her present tension was different than what she had endured before they had reached an understanding. Cord's smile caused it these days, his smile and his good humor and his complete acceptance of the status quo. At times she caught him looking at her with memory in his eyes, but the second she did his expression changed. She had come close several times to blurting out the truth about that night, but something always stopped her, probably humiliation.

"I know he's my husband," she said in a low, taut voice. "But our marriage is in name only. Forgetting that would be begging for heartache."

All hints of levity left Sherry's face. "Oh, Abbie," she sighed. "All this talk about not hoping for more than friendship... You care for him, don't you?"

"I... he confuses me, Sherry. He's kind and considerate and behind every kindness and every consideration is something I can't quite decipher. Most of the time I lay it on what might have happened during... our night together. Sometimes I'm positive he's thinking about it, remembering, and it's so unfair."

"Dammit, tell him you don't remember," Sherry said passionately. "Abbie, why are you afraid to tell him?"

"I don't know. I've tried, but the words get trapped in my throat."

Sherry rubbed her forehead with her fingertips. "You can't let this happen, Abbie. You can't do nothing and let whatever chance you and Cord have slip away. Time goes so fast. Before you know it the baby will be born and it will all be over."

"I can't force something when I'm not even sure I want it, Sherry. I said he confuses me, but that's probably only because he's so different from... from..."

"From the man you thought he was," Sherry prompted. "Yes."

"Will he be a good father? Will you worry when he's taking care of the baby? Will your heart break when he moves out for good? Abbie, *do* something. If you care in the least, do *something*."

Do something. Good advice, but vague, very vague. She couldn't suddenly turn seductive on Cord, especially when she didn't understand her own strange moods. Wooing him seemed ludicrous when their truce—yes, *truce*—wasn't all that solid. Oh, it appeared substantial enough. They could talk now without personal emotion getting in the way. They could discuss their careers, the events of their respective days, the daily news and their pasts like any normal man and woman. They were great at the dinner table these days, even laughing together over nonsensical remarks. Abbie had explained her and Ron Harrison's rivalry, Cord had talked about his friendship with young Danny Atkins, whom he was training. "The boy's a marvel with lighting, Abbie. He's going to be better than I am with portrait photography."

It amazed Abbie that Cord could be humble about his enormously successful career. She had learned through research and concentrated nosiness that a portrait by Cord Durant was regarded as a work of art. Many of his portraits were displayed in prestigious galleries, and those taken home by clients earned him astronomical fees. It was her very ignorance of his reputation that had tipped him off that something was wrong the day she went to his studio, Abbie finally realized, facing, as well, the fact that if she had done her homework prior to that appointment Cord might never have guessed her situation.

It was all water under the bridge, but there was no clarity to their interaction. One minute Abbie thought something important was happening between her and Cord and the next she ridiculed the notion. After all, did he ever even hint at anything beyond a casual relationship for them? Other than those mysteriously arousing shadows she occasionally caught in his marvelous blue eyes, did she have any reason to think he might feel more than friendship for the mother of his child?

That Tuesday Abbie drove home from the station in a pensive mood after her evening broadcast. Lunch with Sherry had only intensified her confusion about Cord. Did she care for him? Did he care for her? Beyond their truce, that is? Beyond their respect for each other's schedules and routines?

When she reached her driveway and the garage door rolled up she saw Cord's car, which she hadn't expected, as he usually spent Tuesday nights in L.A. A fluttering began in her chest and she took a quick peek into the rearview mirror to check her lipstick before getting out.

She opened the connecting door between garage and laundry room and heard music. There was something nice about coming home to music, and she smiled. Going into the kitchen she called, "Cord?"

"In here, Abbie."

Setting her purse on the table, she went on to the living room and then stopped in the doorway, stunned. The room was full of balloons and fresh flowers! "What in the world . . . ?"

Cord appeared from behind a dozen floating balloons. "Happy anniversary, Abbie."

She laughed. "I wondered if you would connect the date. But Cord, all of this wasn't necessary."

"Do you like it?"

"Balloons and flowers? Well . . . I don't know what to say."

"Say you like it. Tell me I'm not an idiot," Cord said teasingly.

"You're not an idiot," she said with a playful swat at a pink balloon, which caused a chain reaction that set every balloon in the room to dancing. Her eyes and lips smiled. The sight was truly delightful. "It's wonderful." She began walking around and inspecting the bouquets of roses and carnations and daisies. "You made some florist very happy." Bending over, she inhaled the scent from a vase of red roses. "Lovely."

"The florist was ecstatic," Cord confirmed with a laugh that faded very quickly. "But it wasn't her happiness I was aiming for."

Abbie straightened. Her heart was doing funny things. No one had ever done anything as impractical as this for her— particularly to mark an anniversary better left neglected— and she felt slightly giddy about it. Her smile was wide and real and warm with affection. "You're a nice guy, Cord."

The air became strangely still, with even the balloons barely bobbing. "Am I, Abbie?"

"Yes," she said, aware of the abnormal breathiness of her voice. "You are." Nervous suddenly, she turned back to the roses. "I didn't used to think you were, you know."

"Yes, I know. Abbie . . ."

He'd come up behind her. Abbie could feel him standing within inches of her back. If he touched her, she feared that she would do something foolish. Some kind of mystical attraction for Cord had developed during the past month, weird ideas that pestered her at night when he was sleeping in the guest room. The mere fact that he was her husband had grown to monstrous proportions, and her curiosity about the night their child had been conceived was becoming an obsession.

Rationally she didn't want their relationship to advance to a physical one, but she was learning that rationality and emotional upheaval didn't always jibe. Fooling around with sex could destroy every gain they had made. At their present level of communication, she would trust Cord with their baby. He was levelheaded and with his priorities in good order.

But this unreasonable attraction was a dangerous business. Their agreement was to divorce when the baby was two months old, and there was no reason to think that any other conclusion would occur. Standing there with Cord just behind her, Abbie faced her biggest fear again: she was afraid of falling in love with Cord.

"Abbie," he said again, and she heard the husky timbre of his voice, the sexually charged emotion behind her name. Until recently, Abbie couldn't have visualized this moment, and it seemed especially fantasy-like now when they were surrounded by balloons and flowers.

"Please, Cord," she whispered, clenching her body in fear that he would touch her. Any physical contact between them since the day she had cried in his arms had been purely accidental. Mostly, they went their separate ways, Cord to his world, Abbie to hers. His sleeping under her roof three or four nights a week was merely for show. They were getting along, as she had told Sherry, and this sort of nonsense had been avoided by both of them.

It wasn't going to be avoided this evening. It was in the room with the balloons and roses and the two of them. It was in the air that Abbie was trying to ingest with studied normalcy so Cord wouldn't sense her inner turmoil, and in the set of her shoulders, in her soul.

"I wanted to make today special for you," Cord said softly.

"You did, but there was...no...reason. I mean, it's really just another day." She tried to laugh. "I can't imagine what you would do for a *real* anniversary."

Cord's mouth tightened. "This *is* a real anniversary, Abbie." He put his hands on her shoulders. "Turn around and look at me."

The telephone rang. Abbie jumped as though struck by lightning, and she had never been happier to hear that often annoying ring in her life. Ducking away from Cord's hands, she hurried to pick up the phone. Her heart was in her throat, but she managed a reasonably normal, "Hello."

An unfamiliar female voice said, "Oh, hello. Is Cord Durant there, by any chance?"

"Why...yes," Abbie said slowly, thinking immediately that her number was unlisted and that Cord must have given it to this woman. The call, of course, was probably about business, although to her knowledge Cord had never received a business call at the house. "One moment, please." Abbie held out the phone. "It's for you."

"Thanks." Cord crossed the room, rippling balloons in the process. "Cord Durant," he said into the phone.

Abbie drifted away through the bouncing, bobbing balloons, intending to leave the room so Cord could take the call in private.

But his discomfiture was immediately obvious, and Abbie stopped just beyond the living-room doorway. "How'd you get this number, Ash?

"But I told Danny not to give it out.

"Well...yeah, guess it's all right, but...

"No, I can't.

"No, Ash, I really can't."

*That* was not a business call! Abbie lifted her chin and took herself to the kitchen and out of hearing range. Literally wringing her hands, Abbie stood at the sink and stared out the window above it. Cord had vowed fidelity all on his own. *She* had suggested nothing more than his discretion. So why did an obviously personal phone call from a woman hurt so much?

Noticing that the oven was on, Abbie left the window and opened the oven door to see a marvelous prime rib browning to perfection. Cord's comments about his cooking ability had been overly modest. He was a much better cook than she was, superb with meat, a magician with vegetables. With only a little training he could have been a chef, which of course was precluded by his love and immeasurable talent for photography.

His talents for that matter, seemed unlimited. He was extraordinarily well-read and well-informed, he followed several sports, he was quite athletic and jogged routinely, his taste in clothing was exceptional, he was handsome and charming and...and...

Tears clogged Abbie's throat and she slammed the oven door closed. Miserable, she went for her purse on the table. It was all too clear that the worst possible scenario for her was happening: In only one month of semitogetherness and absolutely no intimacy, she was falling for her temporary husband.

She started out of the kitchen just as Cord appeared in the doorway. His gaze was steady but unmistakably concerned. "That call was from an old acquaintance, Abbie."

Abbie forced a bright smile. "I thought as much."

"No, you didn't."

"Please don't tell me what I thought about something. You're not a mind reader." Abbie attempted to pass him but he didn't move over and give her enough room. "Please let me by. I'd like to get out of these clothes."

Cord's jaw tensed. "I'd like you to get out of those clothes, too."

A hot flush scorched Abbie's face. "I don't appreciate your crass remarks."

"Abbie, I never gave Ashley Dunn this telephone number."

"But she felt confident in calling, didn't she?" Abbie retorted. "You must have told her that our marriage was just a convenient arrangement."

"I told her nothing. Abbie, I can't stop people from contacting me. Can you? Can anyone?"

"I don't see any men lined up on the doorstep, do you?"

"There isn't a line of women out there, either!"

Abbie looked away. "This is a silly argument. You have the right to do anything you wish, *with* anyone you wish."

"There's only one woman I want to do anything with, and she's standing right in front of me."

Abbie's gaze flashed back to him. Was he serious? His expression was tense, as if he were holding himself in check. Her heart started pounding. He raised his hands and she backed up a step. "No...don't."

"Abbie...dammit." He took a step forward and she retreated another.

"This is...ridiculous," she whispered.

"This is life," Cord muttered. "This is reality, Abbie. We're married. We're living in the same house. On the nights I'm here, do you think I go to bed without thinking of you in the next room?"

"And on the nights you're not here? Who are you thinking of then, Cord?" She had retreated as far as possible; the counter was at her back.

"I try not to think at all." His hands lifted to clasp her upper arms, and she felt the connection with him clear to her toes.

Her eyes became slightly wild. "Cord...why are you doing this?"

"Why do you think?" He inched closer. "Abbie, I keep remembering our one night together. Don't you think about it? Doesn't it nag at you? Gnaw at you? How can you act like it never happened?"

His expression was agitated. The hands gripping her arms were tense. "I...I've tried to forget it," she whispered brokenly, although the truth was on the tip of her tongue. Why couldn't she simply tell him that the night was a blank?

He shook her slightly. "Why?"

"Cord...please don't force something...between us." She saw his jaw clench even tighter. "Don't ruin..."

"Ruin what, Abbie? We walk on eggs around each other. We never talk about anything really important, like that night, for instance." He saw the color rising in her face. "And don't be embarrassed again, dammit! Why shouldn't we talk about it? We made a baby that night. How can you pretend it never happened?"

She was quaking in her shoes, not from the context of Cord's questions but from his proximity, the determination on his face.

"You wrote me off, Abbie," he said darkly. "When you found out about the baby, you never once considered coming to me in an honest, open way and discussing the situation. I'd like to know why you thought pussyfooting around the truth was your only recourse."

Abbie drew a shaky breath. Had these awful questions been simmering behind their bland relationship? What had triggered their release? What, for that matter, had prompted him to go to such extremes to underscore an anniversary that only a truly dedicated couple would even notice?

Resignation seeped into Abbie's befuddled brain: it was time for the bald-faced truth. Her lips parted to speak, to tell him that he had been such a complete stranger to her when she discovered her condition, her only recourse had been deception.

But speaking at all was suddenly impossible, because Cord was kissing her.

# Eight

With her eyes wide open and startled, Abbie registered the curvature of Cord's lips, their texture, their warmth. Shock waves careened through her system, one behind another, arousing her heartbeat to racing speed and weakening her knees.

A small moan built in Abbie's throat. Unbidden, her eyelids drooped, blocking out Cord's face. Some of the kisses of that December night had been in the back of her mind all along, and pinpricks of memory began taunting her.

Cord's arms went around her, bringing her closer. This was the Abbie he remembered. Her soft breasts against his chest nudged memory, holding her without a rein on his emotions ignited desire. She was beautiful, a sensual, sexual woman, and she was his wife. Feverishly hungry for her suddenly, he slid his tongue into her mouth.

She made a small gasping sound and dug her fingernails into his chest. "Abbie...Abbie," he whispered hoarsely and mated their mouths again.

Her mind was spinning dizzily. Her body leaned into his, moved against his, seemingly of its own accord. She could feel the solidity of his chest, his belt buckle, the hot, hard evidence of his desire below it. Her hands wormed around his torso to his back, where her fingertips explored tight, taut muscles and the texture of a summer-weight cotton sweater.

Right, wrong or somewhere in between seemed to have no definition for Abbie, not with Cord's kisses falling on her forehead, her eyelids, her mouth. Her response was as natural as breathing, which didn't feel so natural to her at the moment. Neither was Cord's breathing normal. And yet, despite so many abnormalities to consider, being in his arms felt like coming home. She felt herself flowering, blooming, opening for him, her heart, her soul and certainly her passions.

Not once did she think of refusing. She took his kisses and gave her own, moaned softly at his caresses and reveled in his reactions to her touch.

Her outfit was a loosely structured skirt and blouse. Most of her clothing fit so well, the barely noticeable expansion of her waistline was already straining seams. A shopping excursion was becoming inevitable, as her wardrobe contained only so many garments with a forgiving, comfortable style, such as today's had.

But the slack folds upon her body were convenient for seduction, she realized when Cord's hands slithered beneath her blouse. The thought struck her as delicious, and she laughed deep in her throat.

Cord shuddered as the husky notes raised his blood pressure by several stunning degrees. He claimed another kiss, fitting his mouth to Abbie's, taking her warm breath into his own lungs, absorbing her essence into his very cells. His hands moved beneath the silky fabric of her blouse, encountering lace and satin and smooth skin. He touched her breasts with the utmost gentleness, as he'd heard how tender a woman's breasts could be during pregnancy.

He was burning for Abbie with a fire that had exploded into flames three months before and hadn't been quenched by one night together. Rather, it had been perversely fueled by distance, by frustrating arguments and inane conversations, by the seemingly unbridgeable chasm between them.

That chasm was gone, vanquished by feelings that had grown without any direction from either of them. Things would be fine from here on in, he felt; with this kind of emotion between them, anything was possible.

He wanted to undress her. He ached with the wanting, the needing.

But the kitchen was no place for their first time after so long. Without a word, he withdrew his hands from under her blouse, bent over and scooped her up into his arms. Her expression was slightly dazed, he saw, but her hands went up around his neck. Elated because she'd made no objection, he strode from the kitchen and carried her down the hall and into his bedroom.

He sat on the bed and held her on his lap. Kissing her beautiful swollen lips was imperative. Her response went to his head like a shot of brandy.

But when they broke apart and looked at each other, Abbie whispered, "Should we be doing this?"

"Don't question it," Cord whispered back. "It's right, Abbie. It was right the night we met and it's right now."

It felt right, so wonderfully, excitingly right, that Abbie accepted Cord's judgment. Maybe she could do nothing else, she pondered briefly. Never had she wanted a man more—not that she could remember, at any rate. Obviously he had affected her in just this fashion that night in December. Why else would she have behaved so recklessly?

Cord felt around for buttons on her blouse and found them at the back of its draped neckline, two small nubs that gave easily. All the while he kissed her, caressing her face with his lips. He caught glimpses of her eyes as her lashes rose and fell, and they conveyed a sensual message that warmed his soul.

She twisted then, quite suddenly, and lifted her hands to his hair, whispering "Cord," while her fingertips wove through the dark strands. Abbie felt her natural inhibitions slipping away. It took a few more minutes of increasingly intimate caresses between them, but the utter nakedness of her emotions began to seep into her senses. Cord's kisses were like none she'd ever experienced. The vibrant hunger in her own body would not permit her to leave this bedroom, this bed, without satisfaction.

But a nagging voice in her head advised caution, to not expose every secret portion of herself. They were taking an enormous risk by making love, gambling with each and every gain they had made in the past month. They were not here on this bed because they had fallen so madly in love with each other they could do nothing else. They were in each other's arms because of sexual tension, because there had obviously been a strong physical attraction between them right from the first and it was overwhelming them again. That's what she must never lose sight of. Thinking about love and a permanent future together would be the biggest risk of all.

She stopped thinking at all when she felt Cord's hand under her skirt. Their clothing was awry and bunched, but he eluded awkward wads and located the inches of bare thigh above her hosiery. The union of superheated skin, his palm and the uppermost region of her thighs, jolted Abbie into a gasp.

Cord was surprised. Despite Abbie's obvious and incredibly satisfying response, she seemed slightly shocked by what was only a natural progression to fulfillment. Nothing had shocked her that night in December. He paused briefly to wonder if his memory was faulty. In his mind was a beautiful wanton, a woman who had countered his every advance with one of her own, an aroused, passionate woman who had instigated much of what had taken place between them.

The woman in his arms now, on his lap, breathing huskily and allowing him every freedom, was holding something back. The thought was subtly disturbing, detracting from the excitement Cord was feeling.

But he was too aroused to put a halt to things, especially when Abbie was so cooperative. How odd that she would go so far with him when she wasn't one-hundred-percent sure.

He could get her past whatever hurdle was bothering her, he thought with a sudden burst of confidence. Without their previous encounter to rely on, he wouldn't be so certain, but he knew what she was capable of. He'd felt her passion once before—twice, to be scrupulously accurate—and that was what he wanted from her again, total submersion, unrestrained giving and taking.

He covered her mouth with his and moved the hand under her skirt higher. The strip of her panties between her thighs was easily cast aside, and he felt her shuddering response when he touched her intimately.

"I need all of you," he whispered, and slid her from his lap to the bed. Without hesitation he lifted her blouse over her head and unsnapped the back of her bra. The lacy garment fell away, and the sight of her exquisite breasts stopped him for a moment. "You're so beautiful, Abbie."

She was watching his eyes. Their remarkable color was a deeper blue than usual, appearing lighted by an inner glow. He was an incredibly handsome man. His features weren't precisely perfect if inspected one at a time, but arranged as they were, and enhanced by gorgeous, naturally tawny skin, Cord's face never ceased to startle the female in Abbie. Was it any wonder she had misbehaved at that party? *After* that party?

An intense longing to remember gripped Abbie. He had probably looked at her breasts exactly as he was doing now, with masculine appreciation and unadorned desire in his fabulous eyes. A great weakness stole Abbie's strength. Sitting on a bed naked to the waist beneath a man's admiring gaze felt so strange, but this man was her husband. He wasn't Nick, but he was her husband!

And then Cord raised his hands to her breasts and everything else faded from Abbie's mind. Her nipples puckered and hardened at his gentle, thrilling caresses, and she drew in an unsteady breath.

"I love touching you," Cord whispered. "It's the same for me tonight as it was our first time. Is it the same for you?"

"I . . . think so. Yes . . . of course."

Cord dipped his head to kiss her breasts, wetting one lush, rosy nipple, then the other with his tongue. "You are perfection, Abbie, utter perfection." When her hands came up to his head and her fingers twined in his hair almost roughly, he decided that his thinking about Abbie holding something back had probably been too hasty. There was nothing inhibited in her throaty moans of pleasure, nor in the sensual movements of her body.

Quickly, then, he left her warmth to undress, standing up to shed his clothes. Aware of her watchful gaze, he kicked off his shoes, yanked his sweater over his head, unbuckled his belt, unzipped his fly and pushed down his pants and briefs. Two flicks of his wrist got rid of his socks. Removing his watch, he laid it on the bedstand. Abbie hadn't moved a muscle. He gave her a tentative smile as he returned to the bed.

"Let's get rid of this skirt," he murmured thickly, and began working down her skirt.

She didn't hinder him but neither did she help, and Cord frowned slightly as he untangled the garment at her feet. She had previously slipped her shoes off, but she still wore her hose and panties. The stockings, which he already knew, were those with an elasticized band at their tops instead of garters.

He leaned down and kissed her lips, sensing her instantaneous response with relief. He didn't quite understand Abbie's mood. She had repeatedly and ardently kissed him back—she was doing so now—but she seemed reluctant to act as aggressor, which was so vastly different from their first time together he was having trouble relating that Abbie with this one.

But this Abbie was the lady in his arms, the woman he had to have regardless of more intense memories. Her scent and the smoothness of her skin were drugging. Behind the indisputable desire he had for Abbie was the fact that she was the mother of his baby, which was something he would never find trivial.

Maybe he was holding back a little, too, he pondered, thinking of her condition. Certainly he could never be rough with her now, and there'd definitely been a degree of wildness in their lovemaking last December.

In between kisses that had become heated and needful, Cord rolled down Abbie's nylon stockings. Her mouth was wet and seeking his when her panties were finally drawn down over her ankles and ultimately dropped on the floor.

She was eager for him, he realized with immense satisfaction when he stretched out fully beside her and she wrapped her arms around him. He was driven to arouse her further, to make one final attempt to bring her to that same level of beautiful intensity she had attained so easily at his condo. His mouth left hers and moved downward, lingering at her throat, her breasts, her hipbone. He glanced up at her face and saw that her head was back and her eyes closed; her expression was of another world, one of utter abandonment.

He kissed the insides of her thighs and was about to expand the breadth of his attentions when she squirmed, reached down to his shoulders and urged him to return to his former position. The unspoken but unmistakable restriction startled him—she had imposed no such restrictions during their first time—but he complied by sliding up her body and kissing her on the mouth.

There was no question in Cord's mind about Abbie's desire. Not once during their foreplay had he sensed protestation or denial from her. She wanted what he did, to make love to completion. It was just that—there was no longer any shying away from the truth—somewhere during the past three months, Abbie had developed some disheartening inhibitions.

If he weren't at the point of no return himself, Cord knew that he would close this unsettling chapter of their unsettling relationship with nothing more than some in-depth conversation. But conversation would have to wait; he was close to bursting, and so was Abbie, whether or not her present ideas of making love coincided with memories Cord actually cherished.

Groaning with need and pleasure, he joined their bodies in the ultimate act. She was wet and pliant and completely cooperative, excitingly, beautifully cooperative. Her legs wound around his hips and she moved in a sensual rhythm with him. Cord was soon lost in that other world, enrapt with nothing but the most incredible feeling known to mankind. Abbie was with him every step of the way, with him in the ebb and flow of their bodies, with him in greedy, passionate, wet kisses, with him in hoarsely whispered expressions of pleasure. Doubt vanished as though it had never existed. This was heaven on earth, this was what made one particular man and woman special and unique.

Abbie was weeping and wondering why. Making love with Cord was a trip to the stars. Every nerve ending in her body seemed acutely sensitized and attuned to him. She had felt it all before... with him. The initial event was absent from her mind, but it had happened exactly like this, she knew now. She had lain beneath him, just like this. She had felt her senses expanding to the breaking point and her temperature rising to a searing level. And the tears, falling as though emotions were spilling from her eyes.

She heard her voice, sounding like someone else's, coming out in hoarse gasps, and Cord's, also sounding different than normal. This was not like sex had been with Nick; this was not like anything else in her entire life. She wanted to shout, "Stop! This should not be happening to two people without love! You and I are only married, not in love!"

But she neither shouted nor tried to stop it in any other way. She couldn't. She clung to Cord and wept and let the wave lift her to its crest. At its peak, when everything sensible and solid had melted into sensation, she rode the crest and soared. It went on and on, feeling like the most rapturous of eternities, slowing gradually, until only the beating of her own heart contained remnants of the bliss.

Her tears were drying on her face when next she moved. The man upon her was getting heavy. "Cord?" she whispered.

His head lifted. His eyes, calm and sated, probed hers. A slow smile curved his lips. "Everything okay?"

Her spirit took a massive drop—If only he'd said something tender and meaningful!—but she managed to maintain a relatively impassive expression. "I need to get up."

"Sure, honey, anything." He kissed her lips, brimming with affection for this beautiful lady, and rolled to the bed. With a warm glow, he watched Abbie scooting to the opposite side and yanking the sheet around herself. He smiled again. "You don't need to do that." His smile faded into obscurity when she turned and presented a full view of her face. "What's wrong?"

She didn't know what was wrong. She just felt miserably at odds. "Nothing," she said brusquely, and departed the room like a small tornado, leaving a vacuumlike sensation behind.

Cord sat up with his heart pounding. He'd known something was wrong all along! Dammit, why would she consent to making love if she hadn't wanted to do so?

She *had* wanted to make love; she'd wanted it as badly as he had!

Then what the hell was bothering her? And where had those inhibitions come from? Would he ever understand Abbie? Could anyone ever understand her?

The telephone rang, and Cord shot it a look of pure venom. He let it ring, as he was in no mood to talk to anyone but Abbie. But she was in her bathroom, and the caller was persistent, apparently, because the damned thing kept ringing.

He finally grabbed it. "Hello!"

The phone had rung so many times, Abbie had hurried from the bathroom and came sweeping across the hall in a robe. She reached Cord's room just in time to hear "Don't call me here again, Ash," and to see Cord putting down the phone.

A terrible feeling assailed Abbie. She had just made love with Cord and he had to have a girlfriend. A woman didn't call a man twice within an hour unless there was *something* between them. Abbie was only to the doorway, and she turned to leave, preferring that Cord not know she had overheard the tail end of his conversation.

But he glanced back and saw her. "Abbie?"

She was out of sight now, but sooner or later they would have to face each other with the aftermath of their foolishness: it might as well be sooner.

Abbie came around the door. "Yes?"

"You heard the phone."

"Why did you wait so long to answer?"

"Because I didn't feel like talking to anyone." Cord got off the bed with a disgusted expression and reached for his pants. "I should have let the damned thing ring into oblivion. It was Ash again. I told her not to call me here."

"So I heard. Really, Cord, your girlfriend can..."

Cord uttered a single vicious curse. "She is not—let me repeat—*not* my girlfriend!" He advanced while fastening his pants. "I knew that's what you were thinking. Abbie, I haven't been with another woman since that night in December with you—a date, by the way, that needs some conversation. What happened with you? Why did you take off the next morning like a bat out of hell? Why were you so embarrassed?"

"I don't think I have to explain anything."

"No, you don't have to, but it sure would be a kindness to a man who's been puzzling about it ever since," Cord drawled with some sarcasm. "You're mad at me right now. You got out of that bed mad a few minutes ago, and I'd like to know why. Our making love was a mutual decision, wasn't it? Did I force you into anything? Did I force you into anything last December?"

"I don't know. Did you?"

Cord was only about a foot away from Abbie. His forehead creased with a frown, and he looked her up and down trying to grasp what she'd just said. "What do you mean, did I? Don't you remember?"

Her chin came up. "Actually...no."

Cord's frown deepened. "You're telling me you don't remember the night at my condo?"

"That's what I'm telling you," Abbie said flatly. Oddly, the humiliation she had worried about feeling wasn't anywhere to be found, maybe because she had repeated her mistake with Cord and done it so willingly. What's more, she had recently been thinking silly thoughts about the two of them, and he'd proven how insignificant sex was with her once it was over.

"I don't get it," Cord said, because he couldn't imagine such a monumental memory lapse. "Why wouldn't you remember it?"

"I have no idea," Abbie replied wearily.

The implications began hitting Cord. "My God, no wonder you didn't tell me about the baby! Were you even positive that we had made love?"

"Even without memory I couldn't deny that."

"No, probably not," Cord conceded, recalling the morning after. He'd come out of his bedroom half dressed when he heard Abbie leaving, for one thing. Hell, she had to have awakened naked in his bed! "You really don't remember any of it? Abbie, why didn't you tell me this before? Honey..."

She backed up. "Cord, I want you to leave."

"Leave! Why?"

"Because I'm not going to have an affair with you!"

"An affair! Good Christ, we're married! How can two people married to each other have an affair?"

Abbie's eyes flashed angrily. "Well, what would you call what happened here this evening? Don't play games with me, Cord. You wanted sex, you got sex. No, you didn't force me, but you sure as hell *persuaded* me!" Her expression cooled. "It's not going to happen again. I want you to pack your things and get out of my life. Is that clear enough?"

Fury clenched Cord's jaw. "And the baby?"

"I'll let you know when the baby's born."

"That's not good enough."

"It's all you're getting!" Abbie shrieked. She wilted instantly, stunned by her outburst. "I'm sorry. Just leave. Please. I can't take any more." Turning on her heels, she dashed across the hall to her bedroom and locked the door behind her.

Cord followed. "Abbie, don't do this! I don't deserve this kind of treatment. Talk to me. You're not being fair."

Sitting on the edge of her bed, Abbie hugged her arms around herself and felt the tears starting. "Go away, please."

Cord tried the door. "Abbie, open the damned door!" He had an almost unbearable urge to kick it in, and had to forcibly stop himself from doing so. Discouragement set in then, frustration and anger that making love would end so badly. And that irritating call from Ash couldn't have come at a worse time. Damn all people who wouldn't take no for an answer!

Heaving a sigh, Cord slouched against the wall. Maybe he was as bad as Ash. He sure as hell hadn't ever considered taking Abbie's "no's" as the gospel.

She didn't remember that night. It seemed utterly impossible. She didn't remember the most incredible, burning, wild lovemaking that a man and a woman could possibly devise together.

"Abbie," he called in a calmer tone. "Open the door, honey. Talk to me, please."

Abbie turned around and flopped onto her bed, burying her face in a pillow to stifle the agony of her sobs. She had to be in love with him to hurt so much, but she would die before saying so. What was it he'd said after making love? Oh, yes. *Everything okay?* As though they hadn't just shared the most meaningful of human experiences.

"I don't like you," she whispered raggedly, and then wondered if she was addressing Cord or herself. If she had deliberately set out to destroy her peace of mind last Christmas season, she couldn't have done a better job. Hopping into bed with a stranger, then inviting—inviting—him into something he would never have known about had to be the height of stupidity. The final humiliation was falling for him, returning to his bed, behaving as though she had no mind or will of her own.

"Abbie, I'm going to L.A. for a few weeks." She raised her head from the pillow. "You know how to reach me. Call if you want to talk." There was a silent stretch, and Abbie strained to hear if Cord had gone. But then she heard, "I hope you change your mind…about talking, that is. There's something between us, Abbie, something that could be important. Don't write it off without giving it a chance."

Another pause ensued. "Abbie, I'm not taking my things. Not yet."

Sounds from beyond the door told Abbie the rest: Cord went into his room, got dressed, moved around doing things she could only guess at and returned to the hall. "I'll stay in touch, Abbie. Bye for now."

And then the house was silent, totally, lethally silent.

It was as if Cord's departure had dried up the source of her tears. Hot-eyed, Abbie stared at the ceiling. There was relief in her system, as well as remorse. She could think about loving Cord because she didn't have to face him, which struck her as perverse and unreasonable.

But it was true that she hadn't been exactly reasonable for some time. Neither had Cord. The baby had sent them both into some sort of bizarre orbit. Heaven help them, they had both tried to act normal in abnormal circumstances, but they had failed abysmally and it was best to admit it.

# Nine

___

A phone call from Gary a week later threw Abbie into a tizzy. He was so jolly, so elated to announce a visit to Las Vegas, that she didn't have the heart to burst his bubble.

"I'll let Cord know you're coming," she told him, wondering how she was going to deal with this development. When Gary finally signed off, she sat there stunned for a good five minutes. Her only recourse was to call Cord in L.A., of course. What else could she do? But they hadn't spoken since that fateful evening. He'd talked to her answering machine a few times, and she had listened to his brief messages—*How are you? I'll call again. Take care of yourself*—with her heart in her throat.

She simply did not know what to do about Cord. Hot-and-cold flashes did not constitute a relationship, nor did alternating bouts of relentless remorse and intense wishes that she were the kind of woman to take her pleasure wherever she found it. Sex and love were not separate entities to Abbie, particularly in this constricting situation. Additionally, she had too much feeling for Cord, like it or not, to risk further involvement.

But she couldn't ignore Gary's call or keep it from Cord. There was a lovely bond between the Durant brothers, and Abbie would be the last person to harm such a tie knowingly. Sighing, she got up, located Cord's Los Angeles number, sat down again and dialed it.

There were no guarantees that he would be home at eight in the evening, but he answered on the third ring.

"This is Abbie, Cord."

"Abbie!"

"Please...this isn't about you and me. Gary called. He's coming to Las Vegas and expects to stay here at the house with us."

"Did . . . you set him straight?"

Abbie cleared her throat. "No."

"Any particular reason why you didn't tell him the truth?"

"I thought it should come from you."

"I can't just call him up and lay it on him over the phone, Abbie. You saw him at the wedding. He was like a kid in a candy store. When's he coming?"

"His plane gets in at 12:20 p.m. on Friday. Cord, that's only three days from now. You have to do something. He thinks he's going to be staying here."

"Well, sure he does. Why wouldn't he? Abbie, listen for a minute, okay? I don't want Gary to know what's going on. How long is he planning to stay?"

"For the weekend."

"That's what I thought. I hate asking you for a favor right now, but would you consider letting him think that everything is all right with us? A weekend's not long."

Abbie closed her eyes with a spasm of weakness. A weekend could seem like a year in some cases. "Cord, please don't ask me to do that. You know how I feel, and . . ."

"Abbie, I never told you what Gary did for me."

"You said he took over your care after your parents' fatal accident."

"Yes, but I didn't tell you about the woman he *didn't* marry because of me. They were engaged when our folks were killed, Abbie. So much happened so quickly. Gary had me and our parents' estate to worry about along with his military duties. He took all the time off he had coming and more, risking his career. His fiancée didn't like the idea of a thirteen-year-old kid moving in with them and laid down a few ultimatums. Abbie, Gary chose me over her. I didn't realize it at the time, of course, but in later years I put it all together. Now he's thrilled about my good marriage and I can't..."

"He wouldn't be feeling that way if you had told him the truth right away."

"I honestly don't think he could have accepted the truth," Cord said. "Gary doesn't understand... well, deception. He's the most straight-arrow guy you could ever hope to meet."

"What are you going to tell him when we get a divorce after the baby's birth?"

"Lots of marriages fail, Abbie. But I can't tell Gary we're expecting a baby and planning to get a divorce in the same short weekend."

Almost that exact thought had occurred to Abbie only the day before. Bob Sidwell had returned from his vacation, and she had announced her pregnancy while thinking that she should also be announcing her impending divorce. But the two messages didn't jibe, and she had accepted cheery congratulations while gritting her teeth.

"Abbie, I'll never ask you for another favor," Cord pleaded. "I'd like us to present a solid front. It would only take a few smiles for a couple of days. Please consider doing it."

He was manipulating her again, Abbie realized, this time preying on her sentimentality for a man who had nobly sacrificed his own personal happiness for a kid brother. But her ambivalence wasn't all caused by the Durant brothers' touching background. If she didn't have feelings for Cord, she wouldn't have had an ounce of trouble with a resounding refusal. Like it or not, she was seeing his side of the mess they had made of their lives. Family was crucial to Cord; his determination to stay connected with his unborn child was proof of that immutable trait. Gary was family, Cord's only family at the present if she discounted herself. Putting on an act for one weekend wouldn't kill her.

"Well," she said reluctantly. "I suppose I could try it."

"Abbie, you won't regret it," Cord ardently promised.

Abbie wasn't so certain of that, but she had agreed and would go through with it. Besides, deep within her was the strangest buzz of excitement—just a small clutch of the emotion, but noticeable nonetheless. Talking to Cord was part of it, planning to see him again for a substantial reason was another part. Unquestionably it would be best if she could forget their erotic anniversary celebration. Getting silly with Cord because of a roomful of balloons and flowers really couldn't be construed as anything but another mistake.

But forgetting that episode was as impossible as remembering their first for Abbie. Its intensity struck her with disturbing regularity, coming out of the blue and not always at opportune moments, during a broadcast, for instance, when her mind should be completely free of everything but the information she was passing on to the public.

"I'll be back in Vegas on Friday, Abbie. I'll meet Gary's plane and the three of us will have dinner together," Cord said in her ear, refocusing Abbie's thoughts on the upcoming weekend.

"Fine," she said faintly, recalling that this wasn't at all the result she had hoped for while placing this call. Still, that pocket of excitement floating within her remained intact. At the same time she realized uneasily that there was something she wasn't quite grasping about the weekend, something disturbing but annoyingly obscure. She sighed. It would come to her... eventually. "I'll see you on Friday."

It did come to her, hitting her on Friday morning with the impact of an atomic blast: Gary would be using Cord's bedroom!

Abbie was getting ready for work, and the panic that jarred her into utter chaos was no laughing matter. She dashed across the hall to the guest room only to stare wildly at the closetful of Cord's things. If this charade was going to work, Cord's clothes couldn't be hanging in here!

But if she moved them to *her* closet... ?

She teetered to the room's one chair on rubbery legs and sat down. She hadn't only agreed to put up a front for the

weekend, she had unwittingly agreed to sharing her bedroom with Cord. There was no other place for him to sleep,
and the whole scenario would fall apart anyway if they
didn't occupy the same bedroom. All three of them spending the weekend in Cord's condo would change nothing as
it also had only two bedrooms.

It was too late to back out; Gary was probably already on
his way.

But she had to do something!

Abbie flew to the phone and dialed Cord's L.A. home
number. When there was no answer she called his California studio, which didn't answer either.

Her palms were damp, her heart pounding, but she had
to finish getting ready for work. She did so with fluttering
inefficiency, and at the last minute, just before leaving the
house, she hurried back to the guest room and began un-
loading its closet.


The day was a total bust. Abbie's concentration was
practically nil, and she stumbled twice during her broadcast over simple everyday words, which brought a gleam of
pure pleasure to Ron Harrison's eyes.

The second the broadcast was over, Abbie gathered up her
things and left the station. She had called the house, Cord's
condo and his Las Vegas studio all afternoon, but the only
person she'd reached was Danny Atkins, who had assured
her that Cord was due but that he hadn't yet seen anything
of him.

She headed home, and didn't know whether to laugh or
cry when she saw Cord's car in the garage. The scene looked
serene, precisely what Cord wanted his brother to see, his
car on one side of the garage, hers on the other. Abbie got
out with her lips pursed.

Inside, however, Gary descended upon her with so much
enthusiasm she automatically went into her act. Thoroughly hugged and kissed by her brawny brother-in-law,
Abbie grinned and bore the attention. Gary was bubbling
over because of the baby.

"Cord told me. I'm walking on air, Abbie. Damn, you're pretty, honey. Cord, you devil, you landed yourself the prettiest wife on the whole West Coast." Abbie received another huge hug.

She kept smiling, although she caught Cord's eye and gave him a look that could have curdled milk. He peered around his brother with a perplexed expression and silently mouthed, "What's wrong?"

"As if you didn't know," she mouthed back.

Gary finally let go, and Abbie retreated to another part of the room. "Cord," she said sweetly. "Could I see you in the bedroom for a minute?"

"Sure, sweetheart," he agreed. "Be back in a minute, Gary. Get yourself a beer out of the fridge."

On the trip down the hall, Abbie peered into the guest room and saw Gary's suitcase. She shot Cord another scathing look and continued on to her bedroom, with him right behind her. She closed the door.

"Suppose you tell me how we're going to sleep for two nights," she demanded.

"Abbie, I didn't even think about the sleeping arrangements until I brought Gary's suitcase to my room. By the way, thanks for moving my things. That would have been a dead giveaway."

"I did it this morning, after nearly fainting from panic."

"Then you only thought about it this morning?"

"An enormous oversight," Abbie conceded. "Cord, we can't both sleep in here. Can't you think of something?"

"What? I've been trying, Abbie, but we can't put my brother in a hotel."

"Couldn't he stay at your condo?"

"With what explanation?" Cord was looking at Abbie's bed, which was king-size and beautifully covered with a peach satin bedspread. "That bed could accommodate three or four people."

"That bed is going to accommodate only one person, Cord, the same as it does every other night!"

"Abbie, please. I can't go out there and tell Gary he's not welcome here. I won't touch you, I promise. I'll sleep so close to the edge, you won't know I'm there."

It wouldn't work. Not when the mere thought of sharing a bed with Cord gave her goose bumps. One of them would reach out in the night, one of them would . . .

Weak-kneed, Abbie perched on a chair. "Why do you constantly demand so much from me?" she whispered raggedly.

*Because I'm falling in love with you. Because there's the distinct possibility of having fallen in love with you at first sight.* Cord nearly said it. Holding back took supreme effort. Digesting Abbie's confession about remembering nothing of that night had taken up most of his time since. He understood her better now, if not completely.

He hadn't overlooked the sleeping arrangements as he'd told her. The second she informed him about Gary's visit, he grasped the opportunity just presented him. Abbie's importance was growing by leaps and bounds, and he would use any means he could come up with to keep them communicating.

"I'm sorry," he said quietly. "This will be the last time, I swear it. Abbie, if you do this for me I'll never forget it. You don't know what Gary means to me. He's more father than brother, and he's the best of the best. You saw how excited he is about the baby. What possible good would come out of destroying his happiness? He's going to be a significant influence on our baby's life. Family is . . ."

"All right!" Abbie cried, throwing up her hands. "I give up. But let's get one thing straight, Cord. You *stay* on your side of the bed!"

He smiled. "Oh, I will, honey. Believe me, I will."

Abbie believed nothing at the moment. Later, throughout a very fine dinner in an excellent restaurant, with Gary and Cord beaming at her and referring to the baby in every other sentence, she did come up with one thing to believe, wholeheartedly: she was getting in way too deep with Cord.

He was too damned good-looking. His smiles touched her soul; the adorable way his eyes crinkled at their outer corners when he laughed made her lose her already limited grasp on whatever subject was under discussion. They had all dressed up for dinner, and Cord's pale blue outfit complemented his coloring to the point of indecency. Or maybe, she amended, her own exaggerated sense of indecency was showing. Certainly he was causing her think of how he looked without clothes, and what making love with him was like.

After dinner they took a ride down the Strip. Gary had spent time with Cord in Las Vegas before, but the millions of lights still had him gushing. Abbie couldn't be cool with Gary. He was a peach of a guy, natural with his responses, a bit naive, she thought, but unquestionably sweet.

On the way home he asked about Sherry. Cord immediately suggested that they invite Sherry to join them for dinner tomorrow night, which obviously pleased Gary. Abbie agreed, of course, although she was so tense, she wasn't altogether positive as to what she had just agreed.

Pleading exhaustion at the house, Abbie excused herself and left Cord and Gary in the living room. She showered and got ready for bed, noting the faint hum of their voices when she finally settled down for the night.

Falling asleep was a ludicrous notion, however. Any minute Cord would be walking in as though he did it every night. Gary would be just across the hall, which offered a small measure of comfort as Abbie couldn't believe that even Cord would risk an argument about lovemaking with his brother within listening range.

But an overt pass wasn't what had Abbie worried. She was a lot more concerned about an unintentional collision in the night. If she woke up with Cord wound around her, there was every chance of another big mistake between them. He affected her as no other man ever had. He was sexy and handsome and yes, charming, and she was only human.

She had drowsed in spite of her turmoil, Abbie realized when she awoke with a start as Cord was tiptoeing into the room.

"Sorry," he said quietly. "I didn't mean to wake you."

"It's all right." Abbie registered him going around the foot of the bed and saw that he was wearing only his pants. Her heart took a disconcerting flip.

"I showered in the other bathroom," Cord explained. "Told Gary that I didn't want to disturb you." With his back to the bed, Cord dropped his pants. Abbie caught a glimpse of his briefs before he pulled back the covers and lay down.

"Thanks, Abbie. You were great tonight."

His weight had adjusted the balance of the bed slightly. Abbie stirred to get comfortable again, but she was so aware of Cord on the other side, there was no comfort to be found. There was at least two feet of space between them, but she swore she could feel his warmth.

"Was it terrible for you during dinner?" Cord questioned.

"Terrible? No, I was on edge, of course, but it wasn't terrible. We're going to ask Sherry along for tomorrow night?"

"Gary and I were talking about that. What he'd like to do is ask her to join us for the day."

"The day?"

"Gary wants us all to drive up to Mount Charleston and then tour Red Rock Canyon. You're free, aren't you?"

Mount Charleston and Red Rock Canyon were two of the more scenic areas around Las Vegas. "Well, yes, but..."

Cord turned to his side, facing her, Abbie saw with some trepidation. "It's just tomorrow and tomorrow night left to get through, Abbie. Gary's plane leaves at ten on Sunday morning."

She lay there silently, trying very hard to diminish the sensation of lying in bed in the dark with Cord. She'd put on her least seductive nightgown, a cotton shift without a speck of style or decoration, but a prim gown didn't seem to have much influence on her emotions.

Her heart had started beating ridiculously fast and her mouth was getting dry. She could smell soap and toothpaste and Cord himself, and she knew behind every other thought that if she moved closer to him, he wouldn't shove her away.

"Cord, this is...awful," she whispered. "I knew it would be."

"That's because you and I have never shared a bed without making love," he said softly.

"Don't say that!"

"Why not? It's the truth."

"Sometimes the truth is better left unsaid," Abbie warbled nervously.

"Abbie, I'd like to tell you a story. Will you listen?"

"A story?"

"A very nice story. It's about a man and woman who meet at a party."

"My Lord," she whispered. "No, I will not listen."

"The man had seen the woman before, many times, but only on television. She was even more beautiful in person than she was on the screen."

Abbie covered her ears. "Stop it, Cord."

"That night she was vivacious in a red dress, and she laughed at everything the man said, as though she thought him wonderful, witty and wise. He fell a little bit in love with her while they danced. She felt incredible in his arms and he couldn't touch her enough."

Tears burned Abbie's eyes. "Why won't you stop?"

Cord heaved himself up to an elbow. "Because this is a story you have to hear, Abbie. You won't know what I do until you hear it all."

"What...do you know?"

"That something important began that night. Abbie, please listen."

"It's too...embarrassing," she whispered.

"Making love is *not* embarrassing, Abbie. Where did you ever get that idea?"

"You're not the one who woke up in a strange bed with no memory of what had put you there!"

"No, but that's exactly what I'm trying to rectify."

Abbie turned her back to him and sighed wearily. "Please just go to sleep, Cord. Let's not make this more difficult than it already is."

Cord slowly lay down again. "You know," he said quietly, "I'm sure that every person has one very special memory. That night is mine, Abbie. I was mystified—and hurt—about the morning after. To save my soul I couldn't figure out why you left the way you did. We made love twice, Abbie, and I don't mind telling you that I fell asleep after the second time thinking about a vastly different kind of morning than what actually took place."

"But you know it all now," Abbie said, her voice thick with unshed tears. "And talking about it wouldn't change a thing. Our reality isn't very pretty, Cord. Mine, in particular."

"Abbie, you're denouncing yourself for being human."

"I'm denouncing myself because I went to bed with a man I didn't know."

"You know me now."

Abbie raised her head. "Yes, and you're not especially pretty, either. If I went to bed with a man I didn't know, you did exactly the same with a woman you didn't know."

"We knew each other a hell of a lot better than you're giving us credit for, Abbie. I happen to possess a very clear mental picture of that night, and we did nothing wrong."

A desire to know the whole story had started burning a hole in Abbie. Would he tell it discreetly? Graphically? Romantically?

"Do you remember my Christmas tree?" Cord asked.

Abbie stiffened as a door in her mind opened a crack. His Christmas tree! Why would she remember that now with such a trivial reminder? Would she remember the rest of the night with a few more nudges to her memory?

She turned over again to lie on her back. "I do remember your tree, or I think I do. It was a live tree, wasn't it?"

"I always buy a living tree," Cord concurred. "When the season's over, I give it to someone to plant in their yard. This year Danny took the tree. It's growing beautifully, incidentally."

"And you hadn't finished trimming it," Abbie said slowly, thoughtfully.

"That's right. There were decorations strewn all over the living room. You found a length of silver tinsel. Do you remember what you did with it?"

Abbie was remembering more than tinsel. Cord had kissed her in the elevator, in the corridor, in his foyer, and he then followed her around his living room while she exclaimed gaily about his Christmas decorations.

"I . . . strung it around my neck like a necklace," she said tremulously.

"Then what happened, Abbie?" Cord questioned softly.

*She took the tinsel from her own neck and wrapped it around Cord's. He laughed and caught her to himself, seeking her mouth with his.*

*The passionate kiss made her feverish with excitement. The tinsel streamer fell to the floor, forgotten.*

*They sank to the carpet. Clothes were discarded fast and furiously, her dress, his coat and shirt. Without even losing every stitch, she pulled Cord on top of her, kissing and holding him with an almost desperate hunger. "Make love to me, Cord, oh, please make love to me."*

She had said that to him. She had actually *begged* him, a total stranger, to make love to her! Not that he'd been waiting for an invitation. His hands had been everywhere.

But so had hers. Abbie's face flamed in the dark. No wonder he had accused her of being all over him!

"The first time was wild," Cord whispered. "The second . . ."

"Don't!" Abbie interjected. "I've remembered enough to get the general idea."

It struck Cord that Abbie's attitude wasn't being influenced by what she was remembering. He had hoped she would feel as much affection for that night as he did, once she knew how beautiful it had been.

She simply did not grasp the beauty of total and complete sexuality, he decided, and it was time to set her straight on that most crucial of points.

He slid across the vacant space in the bed. Taking Abbie by surprise, he gathered her into his arms. But he didn't kiss her startled mouth. Instead he peered into her face at close range. "I want you to listen to me. You were incredible that night, do you hear me? You were free and beautiful and not afraid of anything. You never once slowed us down with objections, and you met me more than halfway. Abbie, last week our lovemaking was wonderful, I can't deny that. But it was different than our first time. Do you recognize the difference?"

She was stunned to near speechlessness. Cord was not only holding her when he'd promised to stay on his side of the bed, he was demanding an intimacy of communication that only true lovers could possibly attain. If she made a fuss, Gary would hear. If she didn't, anything might happen. One of Cord's legs was thrown over hers. His most intimate parts were pressed into her hip, and unquestionably he was becoming aroused.

"You can't make me talk about this," she whispered frantically. "And you promised to keep your hands to yourself."

"Do you know what you're doing to us, Abbie?"

"What *I'm* doing?"

"Do you have any feelings at all for me?"

Tears sprang to Abbie's eyes. "Why are you talking about feelings? Cord, our marriage is a sham. Do you want me to tell you that you affect me physically? You know you do without my saying so. Our agreement..."

"*Screw* the agreement!" Cord's voice dropped again. "Make love with me, Abbie, like you did the night our baby was conceived."

"Gary..."

"Gary thinks we're madly in love. Why wouldn't we *make* love? You were right about this bed, Abbie. It's not big enough for the two of us to be in it without getting some very exciting ideas. My ideas are to..." Cord put his mouth to her ear "...give you pleasure, sweetheart. Let me. You know I can do it."

His hand slid down her body, going beneath the sheet and blanket. Abbie shivered. "I'm putty in your hands, aren't I?" she whispered. "You knew this would happen."

His lips began moving over her face, while his hand under the covers located the hem of her sedate nightgown and slipped beneath it. "Abbie," he whispered. "We've got a ways to go yet, but we're a couple, honey. Our marriage isn't completely a sham."

Wasn't it? Abbie was fast losing her resistance to making love with Cord again. He knew the most delicious ways to tantalize a woman, like sliding his fingertips up and down her naked thighs. In the next instant his mouth possessed hers, and her final resistance disappeared in a maelstrom of passion.

Her returned kiss was as hungry as Cord's. Dimly she wondered how his briefs could contain the power of his arousal, but he must have been thinking the same thing, because in one fluid movement the underwear vanished from his body.

They became impatient with kisses and caresses very quickly. Forgetting about Gary sleeping just across the hall and that she had vowed to avoid another such session with Cord, Abbie urged him on top of her. She whispered against his lips, "Make love to me. I need you."

"Again and again," Cord whispered, promising endless pleasures to his lady.

If she was wanton, so be it, Abbie thought dreamily when he was doing precisely as she had asked. Her nightgown had been whisked over her head, her naked breasts were being tormented by his chest and the friction of Cord's body moving in hers was the height of ecstasy.

She rose to the peak very quickly, breathing hard, clinging and rocking beneath her lover...her *husband*. She never quite lost sight of who he was, did she? she thought. There was something magical about their marriage, travesty or not.

But would it last? The question remained in the back of her mind behind the dizzying, dazing pleasure of completion and the soft, mewling cries she couldn't prevent. It surfaced again when Cord had quieted and she was lying beneath him in the still, glowing aftermath of mutual satisfaction.

*Would it last?* How could it with such an ignominious beginning and a solid agreement to end it on a predetermined date?

Later, after they had taken turns refreshing themselves in Abbie's bathroom and were back in bed, Cord snuggled close with a murmured, "It could be like this every night, Abbie."

She didn't ask him to move over, but neither did she agree with his sleepy comment. Something inside her felt ripped apart by conflicting attitudes. She was falling in love, and maybe Cord was, too. But neither of them had said so, nor had they talked about terminating their divorce agreement.

Making love could easily become a habit. But it would pull her deeper and deeper into a one-sided commitment. She was already getting very close to some serious heartbreak at the cessation of this arrangement; unrestrained lovemaking for its remainder would guarantee her unhappiness.

It had to end now, while she was still capable of a modicum of clear thinking.

# Ten

———

Cord awakened to an empty bed in the morning. Abbie, apparently was already up and out of the master suite as there was no sound in the bathroom. A lazy smile tipped the corners of his mouth as he remembered the previous night. Abbie had been the woman from his special December memory—excited, sensual and unabashedly in need of him. Granted, their activity had been restricted because they weren't alone in the house, but it was immensely satisfying to know how strongly he affected her.

He wished with a sigh that she hadn't gotten up before him. If she were still in bed with him, he would make long, slow, delicious love to her. Maybe they could talk about the future, as well. Afterward, of course. First things first, he thought with purely masculine amusement.

The amusement vanished. The future was serious business. That damned agreement had to be destroyed. There were months left to accomplish its destruction, but he had no defined instinct about Abbie's compliance. Yes, he had the power to lead her into making love with him, and yes, she was gradually warming toward him on other levels. But she was a strong-minded woman and stubborn, to boot. He hadn't exactly ingratiated himself with his premarital demands about the baby, although he would never regret forcing that issue. The thought of his baby gave him a feeling like no other he'd ever experienced. Friends had told him about the melting love one felt for one's own children, but he hadn't been able to fully grasp their meaning of that until recently.

It was just so damned sad that Abbie hadn't been able to come to him with the news in a forthright manner. He understood now why she'd felt so alone, but understanding her attitude didn't eradicate sorrow for him.

They had gotten off to a bad start. Actually, they had gotten off to a great start, but she barely remembered it, and what she did remember were the mechanics of their first night together, not the emotions. If she would listen, he'd give her every detail, which he had no trouble at all in recalling.

*They were lying on the living-room carpet. Her dress and panties were gone but sheer hosiery was still covering the fabulous long legs wrapped around him. Her bra was half on, half off, his mouth was darting back and forth between her rigid nipples and her soft, eager lips. He'd never felt so much desire from a woman before. She was a fever in his blood, causing a roar in his head. "Abbie... Abbie..."*

*"Cord, oh, Cord." Her voice was husky and from the bottom of her throat.*

"Damn," Cord muttered, realizing that memory was arousing him to the point of discomfort. Throwing back the sheet and blanket, he swung his feet to the floor. He couldn't go and find Abbie, not in broad daylight with Gary in the house. A cold shower was due about now.

Abbie refilled Gary's coffee cup at the kitchen table. He sent her a warm smile. "Thanks."

"You're welcome." She sat down to her cup of hot tea. "What do you like for breakfast?"

"What do you and Cord usually have?"

Abbie hesitated. She and Cord had never once eaten breakfast together. When he stayed at the house, their mornings didn't quite coincide. He left for the studio earlier than she left for the station, and mornings by their very nature were hectic. "Um…not much, actually. Fruit for me and cold cereal or a piece of toast for Cord." She smiled. "But this is a special occasion. How about some blueberry pancakes and crisp bacon?"

"Sounds like a treat to me," Gary laughed. "I live on base these days, and while military grub isn't quite as bad as you might have heard, it can't compare to home cooking." After a sip of coffee, he laughed again. "Looks like Cord's sleeping in. That's okay, though, Abbie. Gives us a chance to talk. I'm so doggone happy for the two of you, I feel silly. A baby. You know, I don't really care if it's a boy or a girl, but wouldn't it be something if Cord had a son?"

"And you had a nephew?" Abbie teased with a truly affectionate smile. Gary Durant was like a big, lovable, floppy-eared puppy. Not that he wasn't good-looking. It was just that he had such an open, giving personality, as if he were happily looking out for the rest of the human race. If anything came of his and Sherry's budding friendship, Sherry would have a man who was an exact opposite to the petty, mean-minded husband she had finally divorced a few years back.

Gary's grin was slightly guilty. "A baby girl would be great, too, Abbie. Cord's a lucky man. A wonderful wife and a baby on the way. Yeah, he's a lucky guy."

Cord might debate that opinion, Abbie thought, although she said quietly, "He told me you were engaged once, Gary. I'm sorry it didn't work out."

"Yeah, well, things happen, Abbie. I've never come right out and talked to Cord about it, but my fiancée wouldn't accept my decision about him living with us. She wanted me to put him in a foster home. It wasn't even an option, as far as I was concerned. My own brother? He was thirteen years old and devastated. I couldn't desert him, not for love or money."

"Cord knows," Abbie said simply.

After a moment Gary nodded. "Guess he figured it out on his own."

"Hey, you two early birds," Cord exclaimed as he strode into the kitchen.

Abbie glanced up and saw him descending upon her. She lifted her cheek and intercepted a kiss that she knew had been aimed at her lips. "Morning, sweetheart," Cord said softly.

"Good morning," Abbie murmured. Gary's expression, she saw from across the table, and with an inward sigh, was one of great joy. The man was in seventh heaven because of his younger brother's marital bliss. "There's fresh coffee in the pot," she told Cord.

"Great," he remarked while moving to the counter with the coffee pot. He poured himself a cup and glanced out the window. "Looks like a beautiful day out there."

"Why don't the two of you enjoy your coffee on the patio while I make breakfast," Abbie suggested while getting to her feet.

"And leave you with all the cooking?" Cord turned. "Why don't we go out for breakfast?"

"Thanks, but I promised Gary some homemade blueberry pancakes. Go on, both of you. You've still got a lot of catching up to do. I don't mind cooking breakfast in the least." Abbie checked the time. "In fact, if you're still thinking of asking Sherry to go with us today, someone had better go over there and do it before she decides to take off for parts unknown."

Gary got up. "I'll do it right now. See the two of you in a few minutes."

And just like that, Cord and Abbie found themselves alone. He set down his cup and walked over to her. She was wearing a sundress with splashy lavender-and-fuchsia flowers along with green leaves and sprigs on a white background. Her sun-streaked blond hair was gleaming, her lips glossy and pink.

He rested his forearms on her shoulders in a casual pose. "You're as pretty as a picture this morning, Mrs. Durant."

Abbie's breath stopped in her throat. "Cord . . . we have to talk."

"Yeah, we do. Last night was fantastic, wasn't it? I woke up this morning thinking about it and wishing you were still in bed with me." He smiled lazily and tenderly brushed a strand of hair from her cheek. "I took a cold shower, but right now it seems like a totally wasted effort."

The easiest course, Abbie thought unhappily, would be to allow herself to be swept along by Cord's mellow, sensual mood. He was incredibly handsome with his damp hair and shower-shiny skin, and his scent alone was enough to drive a woman to the brink.

But this couldn't go on. She couldn't wilt and whimper every time he touched her, not if she hoped for a reasonably sane conclusion to this mad liaison. A plan was beginning to take shape in the back of her mind. Now wasn't the time to mention it, but when Gary's visit was behind them Cord was going to have to hear and accept it.

Abbie ducked away from him. "I have to start breakfast."

He trailed after her, trying to pull her into his arms. "There's no hurry, sweetheart. Hold still and let me kiss you." And then he caught on that she wasn't only playing coy with him this morning. "What is it, Abbie?"

"Please don't ask me to explain right now. I'd like to delay this conversation until after Gary leaves." She began pulling the ingredients for blueberry pancakes from a cabinet.

The cold-water shower hadn't been nearly as effective as Abbie's mood. Cord had honestly envisioned their relationship on an upward swing. Apparently Abbie could make meaningful love at night and blueberry pancakes in the morning with the same amount of commitment.

"Fine," he said coolly. "We'll talk after Gary leaves." Picking up his cup of coffee, he went through the French doors and out to the patio. He walked around the side of the house so Abbie couldn't see him from the kitchen window. He wanted to throw something, but instead cursed violently under his breath.

* * *

The Mount Charleston area was green, cool and beautiful. Rising from the arid desert floor, the treed mountains offered relief from heat, smog and congestion, and were a favorite playground for the city dwellers from the valley. Cord stopped at the resort for lunch, and Gary and Sherry enjoyed the excellent food and great view immensely. They thought it a big joke that their names rhymed and made such a to-do about it that even Cord and Abbie laughed.

But Cord and Abbie weren't in the same merry mood as their companions, although they covered their uneasiness so well Gary didn't catch on. Sherry was another matter, however, and Abbie knew that her friend's keen eyes were missing none of her tension or Cord's.

From Mount Charleston they drove to Red Rock Canyon. Cord parked near a trail and they all got out of the car. The area was striking, with unusual rock formations, and many nature lovers went out there to hike and climb the challenging slopes and cliffs.

Abbie felt a little tired and asked to be excused from the hike the two men had enthusiastically planned during the drive. Cord was instantly concerned. "Abbie, do you feel all right?"

"I'm fine, Cord, really. I just don't feel like hiking. But the three of you go and enjoy yourselves."

"I think I'll stay here with Abbie," Sherry said firmly.

Cord, Abbie could see, was losing interest in the hike. "Please," she said directly to him. "Go with Gary and have a good time. Sherry doesn't have to stay behind, either."

"But Sherry *wants* to stay behind," Sherry said with a twinkle in her eye. "Save me, Abbie. You know I detest hiking."

Finally the two men took off down the trail. Abbie sighed when they were out of earshot. "This is getting sticky. I know you caught on that all is not well with Cord and me, but do you think Gary did?"

"Not in the least," Sherry said reassuringly. "Let's sit in the shade on that big rock over there." When they were settled out of direct sunlight she asked, "Do you feel like talking about it, Ab?"

"I've been getting more mixed up by the day," Abbie admitted wearily.

"You poor kids," Sherry said softly. "Talk about starting out with two strikes against you. Abbie, I know you care about Cord, and darn it, he cares about you, too. Look how quick he was to worry when you said you didn't feel like hiking."

"He worries about the baby, Sherry, not me."

"Are you really so sure about that?"

Abbie looked away. "I'm sure of nothing." Her eyes came back to her friend. "Except for one thing. I've got to break this up before I get in so deep I'll never get over it."

"You're in love with him."

"I'm close. Think of my house, Sherry. Gary is using the guest room."

Sherry's face fell. "And Cord slept . . . with you?"

"Where else? He's got this . . . this obsession about keeping Gary in the dark about our arrangement. I foolishly agreed to the pretense before giving the limited sleeping space any thought." Abbie got up and paced a small circle. "It got all out of hand."

"But you didn't . . . I mean, you only slept, didn't you?"

Abbie's cheeks got pink, and she couldn't quite look Sherry in the eye. "I'm putty in his hands, which I told him, for all the good that will do."

"Apparently your conversations go only so far," Sherry said sadly. "Oh, Ab, you've been my friend for a long time and you'll always come first, but I like Cord, too. I feel bad for both of you."

Abbie returned to the boulder and sat down again. "Do you know what I'm most afraid of, Sherry? That Cord is confusing wanting me with wanting his baby. There's no comparing Cord and Nick, nor the circumstances, but I don't think I could face another bad ending."

"You've had your share of unhappiness. No question about it. Well, as I told you before, I'll support whatever you decide to do."

"I made one small decision this morning," Abbie said evenly. "You know that folding cot in your spare room? I'd like to borrow it for tonight."

* * *

By that afternoon everyone had agreed to barbecuing steaks on Abbie's grill for dinner instead of eating out. Sherry contributed to the meal from her own kitchen and together the two women prepared a huge tossed salad and corn on the cob. Cord again proved his wizardry with meat and turned out perfect medium-rare steaks.

They ate at the table on Abbie's patio, raving over their own fine cooking. Everyone but Abbie added an excellent red wine to the menu, but she was content with her stemmed glass of fruit punch.

"Cord, I have to have a picture of this to remind me of today," Gary exclaimed.

Cord froze. "I . . . don't have a camera, Gary."

Abbie jumped in. "Sure you do, Cord. The one in that small cabinet in the den?"

"Oh, *that* camera," Cord said, and hurried into the house while wondering what in heck kind of camera Abbie owned. It turned out to be a thirty-five millimeter with a built-in flash, not the high-quality equipment he was used to working with, but not bad. He checked and saw that it already contained film, so he went outside smiling.

Everyone made silly faces, but he snapped half a dozen shots before resuming his place at the table.

"What about the pictures of your wedding?" Gary questioned. "I'd like to see them."

Cord and Abbie exchanged glances. "They're still at the studio," Cord replied.

Gary turned to Abbie. "You mean that you haven't seen them, either?"

"No . . . but I will," she said quickly. "Cord promised to bring them home this week."

"Well, for Pete's sake," Gary declared. "Don't the two of you realize how precious those photos will be in a few years?"

"Precious . . . yes." Abbie smiled weakly. "Would you like another ear of corn, Gary?"

The meal was a success despite the discomfiting photo conversation. Everyone pitched in to clean up, then returned to the patio to watch the sun go down.

"Ever use that pool?" Gary asked.

"All the time in hot weather," Abbie said.

"How hot does it have to be?" Gary laughed. "Mind if I use it?"

"Go right ahead," Abbie told him.

"Anyone else interested?" Gary inquired while looking at Sherry.

"Sure, why not?" she replied.

"I'll pass," Cord said. "Unless you want to take a swim, Abbie."

"No, not tonight. But you all go ahead."

Sherry ran over to her house to change and Gary went in for his bathing suit, which he announced that he'd brought with him just in case.

The patio was suddenly silent. The sun was behind the mountains and the air was silvery and cool. During the flurry of dinner preparations, Sherry had brought over her folding cot and Abbie had tucked it in her closet. She wondered if this was the moment to mention the vastly different sleeping arrangements for tonight.

"Thanks for thinking fast on that camera thing," Cord said quietly.

Abbie put the cot issue on hold. "I like Gary, and if you prefer him not understanding our situation at this point it's okay with me."

"I appreciate it."

"Our... divorce is going to be hard on him, isn't it?"

"Hard on everyone," Cord said grimly. "I don't even like thinking about it."

Abbie's head snapped around. "You don't?"

Cord got up and leaned against a patio post, shoving his hands into his pants pockets. "Do you know anybody who would?"

"Well, you're certainly not happy now, are you?"

Cord looked off at the final faint pink streaks of the sunset. "No, I can't say I'm particularly happy right at the moment." He glanced back over his shoulder at her. "Are you?"

Abbie lowered her eyes to her hands. "No." An ache in her heart threatened her feeble grasp on composure. "But we didn't get into this for our happiness, did we?"

"Ultimately, yes," Cord rebutted, thinking of the baby coming in September. What greater happiness could a man have than to witness the birth of his own child? "But I didn't know how tough it was going to be."

"I did. Why did you think I fought you so hard? Even a good marriage puts enormous pressure on people, Cord."

"And your first marriage was good."

"For a short while, yes. Until we learned of Nick's illness, it was very good."

Cord sighed. "Hard for another man to compete with that kind of memory, isn't it?"

Abbie was about to object to his reference to "competition" when Gary came out. Clad in a dark bathing suit, he exclaimed, "Sherry isn't back yet?"

"Sherry's back," came a voice out of the growing darkness. Sherry came around the back of the house and onto the patio.

Abbie saw Gary's face light up at the sight of Sherry in a white bathing suit. She looked great, Abbie thought, just great, and Gary was definitely interested. How ironic it would be if Cord's brother and her best friend should become seriously involved.

While Gary and Sherry ran for the pool, Cord sat down in the chair next to Abbie's. "Can we talk? They won't hear us if we keep our voices down."

"Yes," Abbie said, thinking of that cot in her closet again, which was bound to come as a shock to Cord after last night.

"You don't *want* to like me, do you, Abbie?"

"I...what?" Abbie turned amazed eyes on him. "Whatever gave you that idea?"

"What else should I think? When we make love you're one woman and immediately after you're someone else. It doesn't take a Ph.D. in human relations to understand that you keep going through some kind of transition from passionate to regretful. You're physically attracted to me, I

know that. What I don't know and can't begin to compre-
hend is why you're so damned sorry afterward.''

Abbie was stunned. Cord wasn't the least bit dense, but
his summation of their bizarre relationship was appalling.

''Do you really expect me to believe that you have no hint
about why I keep retreating?'' she questioned. ''Dammit,
Cord, sex between any two people locked into an arrangement such as ours is ridiculous. We're not kids and we're not
irresponsible, either of us. To put it bluntly, we shouldn't be
playing around!''

Abbie stood up. ''I'm going to say good-night to our
guests and call it a day.''

Ignoring the stunned look on Cord's face was impossible, but Abbie hurried over to the pool and bid her guests
good-night. ''I've got some technical reading for work to
catch up on. Hope you don't mind.'' Her excuse wasn't a lie;
she always had stacks of reading awaiting attention, what
was happening in local politics, in the police department,
with the Clark County school board and the University of
Nevada's board of regents, who was in command, who had
stepped down and for what reason. Staying informed was an
important part of her job, and she'd always made a consci-
entious effort to comply.

Not that she really planned to read tonight. She was tired,
not exhausted or feeling ill, but tired. And anxious for tomorrow, when she could stop pretending and get back to
normal. Gary was a great guest and she truly liked him, but
entertaining was doubly draining with the strain of so much
pretense.

Instead of her usual quick bedtime shower, Abbie soaked
in the tub for a good long spell. With her head back and her
eyes closed she took a stab at critical self-analysis. Was the
plan she was going to present to Cord after Gary had gone
unrealistic? Was the tremendous need she felt to protect
herself against future grief selfish? Had she really been as
fair to Cord as she could have been? Should she censure
Cord for wanting sex, when the chemistry between them was
so overwhelming?

In some ways Abbie knew she was wavering. Love was not
a rational or logical emotion. One didn't plan to fall in love,

one merely bungled one's way into it. And *fall* was an appropriate word, because the feeling was similar to losing one's footing.

Except it wasn't always like that, Abbie amended with a forlorn sigh. When love was returned and shared and nurtured, when lovers were without pretensions or guardedness, love was the most splendid of human expressions.

Dear God, Abbie thought wearily, she was getting so philosophical her head was beginning to ache. From outside came the drift of voices, Gary's, Cord's and Sherry's, and laughter. They were probably finishing the dinner wine and enjoying the cool night air.

Abruptly, though, everything became silent. Quickly Abbie got out of the tub and dried off, taking a minute to apply body lotion. But the quiet of the house had to indicate the conclusion of the evening and she hurried, as Cord was bound to come into the master suite at any moment.

Wearing a nightgown and robe, Abbie opened the bathroom door. A small lamp was burning and Cord was sitting on the foot of the bed. "Hi. Gary saw Sherry home." He smiled slightly. "I don't expect him to immediately return."

Abbie licked her suddenly dry lips. "Probably not. They seem to be getting along very well."

"They are. Makes me realize what we missed, Abbie."

His eyes looked dark in the dim light, dark and speculative and wary. Abbie realized that he didn't know what to expect from her now, which created a terribly sad void in her system and a desire to soothe him.

But consoling Cord would lead directly to the middle of that king-size bed, and whether she was right or wrong, selfish or merely sensible, biased or the most scrupulously impartial of women, she was not going to make love with him again. Not with that despicable, treacherous agreement hanging over their heads, she wasn't.

She went to her closet and began wheeling out Sherry's folding cot. Cord stood up. "What's that?"

"I borrowed it from Sherry. It's a cot, and I'm going to sleep on it tonight." Abbie released the cot's restraints and unfolded it near the window. "It's not big enough for you," she added.

"If you think I'm taking your bed while you sleep on a damned cot, think again," Cord snarled, instantly angry.

"For crying out loud," Abbie said disgustedly. "There's nothing wrong with me sleeping on this cot, so stop with the macho attitude!"

"I don't have an attitude!"

"Like hell you don't!" Abbie yanked clean sheets out of a drawer and slapped them down on the cot.

"You're pregnant!"

"Pregnancy doesn't make me fragile! Besides, this cot is perfectly comfortable. It's got a darned good mattress."

Cord was pacing, watching her yank the sheets into place. "I'm not taking your bed."

"You took it last night," Abbie pointed out. "What's different about tonight?"

"You were in it! Abbie, *I'll* sleep on the cot."

Abbie sent him a disgusted look. "Your feet would hang over the end. Cord, don't be silly. Go to bed." Getting a pillow from a shelf in her closet, Abbie tossed it toward the head of the cot. "That's where I'm going, and I'd appreciate a little peace and quiet around here, if you don't mind."

Cord had heard just about enough. He put his hands on his hips and regarded her through narrowed, furious eyes. "Lady, after tomorrow morning you're going to have *lots* of peace and quiet."

Turning slowly, Abbie faced him. "Meaning?"

"I've had enough. You can let me know when the baby's born."

Abbie's chin came up. "That's precisely what I was going to suggest—*again,* by the way—after Gary leaves."

"We agree, then. I'll take my things back to my own place."

"Yes, we agree."

Cord whirled and stalked into the bathroom, closing the door with a lot more force than it needed. Abbie wilted, sinking to the little cot. The "darned good mattress" felt like a rock, and she gave it an ineffectual punch and blinked at the tears stinging her eyes. She hurt. She hurt so much she wondered if she would ever *stop* hurting.

Falling in love with the wrong man was the bitter end.

After a shower, which calmed him some, Cord returned to the bedroom in just his briefs, prepared to instigate another conversation—this one, hopefully, to undo the damage of the other. The small lamp was still on. Abbie was on the cot with her back to the room.

Anger returned to clench Cord's jaw. He had no choice. It was either bed down in here or do something he'd regret later, like marching over to Sherry's house, interrupting Gary's courtship with a very sad story and driving to his condo for the night.

After a minute of silent seething, he climbed into Abbie's king-size bed, snapped off the lamp and settled down.

He knew she wasn't sleeping yet, but he couldn't think of one thing to say that wouldn't start another fight.

# Eleven

Cord and Sherry drove Gary to the airport after Abbie had made a number of good-natured promises to her brother-in-law. Yes, I'll stay in touch. *Yes, I'll make sure Cord sends the pictures he took last night the minute they're developed. And copies of the wedding pictures. Yes, I'll take care of myself.*

Then everyone was gone and the house was suddenly silent, empty and feeling much bigger than it was. Abbie sat at the kitchen table and sipped from a cup of herbal tea while pondering the weekend. It seemed to her that Cord was making a big mistake by keeping the truth from Gary. Her brother-in-law impressed her as a mature, responsible individual. Gary didn't need his younger brother living a lie for his benefit.

She never should have agreed to the weekend charade. What good had come out of it? Obviously Cord was an opportunist, taking advantage of a situation even after making an adamant promise to do otherwise. They had both ended up hurt.

Abbie heaved a despondent sigh. Cord was probably going to move his things when he got back from the airport. She thought about him hauling his clothes out to his car and realized that she didn't want to see it. What would she say? What would *he* say?

No, she definitely did not want to be on the premises when he returned. Bringing her cup to the sink, Abbie got her purse from her bedroom and went out to the garage. She drove away with no destination in mind.

Cord parked his car in the driveway, and Sherry got out and went to her own house. He walked through Abbie's front door calling her name. It took him about ten seconds to register her absence, but he went from room to room anyway, to make sure she wasn't merely avoiding him.

She was avoiding him, all right, he thought grimly. So much so that she had left the house to accomplish it.

It was over, truly and painfully over. If Abbie had had the slightest inclination to repair their splintering relationship, she would have been here.

Cord stood in the master bedroom and glared at that miserable cot. He hadn't slept worth a damn and neither had Abbie. He'd heard her squirming half the night, which would serve her right if he didn't think it was important for a pregnant woman to get a good night's sleep.

But then he had to admit that Abbie wasn't completely wrong about last night's sleeping arrangements. He shouldn't have made a pass that first night in her bed, even if it had felt infinitely right at the time.

Cord went into the bathroom and began gathering up his shaving gear. He stopped to look himself in the eye in the mirror and question what he really wanted from Abbie. Was he in love with her? Oh, he loved her, make no mistake. But any man loved a woman who made him feel so good in bed. Being in love was a whole other ball game. Had he ever been really in love in his life?

Love was a strange emotion. Without question he already loved his child. He had loved his parents and certainly his feelings for Gary had to be in the ''loving'' category. But there were so many subtleties connected with love, so many variations on the same theme.

He had recognized last night that he and Abbie had missed what Gary and Sherry were getting giddy over, the flirting, the teasing, the exchanged glances, the covert touching. In a private conversation this morning, Gary had confessed a deep attraction to Sherry. "We really like each other, Cord. We have so much to talk about. We really enjoy each other's company, even when we're not talking."

Maybe that was the underlying problem with him and Abbie, Cord thought. They hadn't taken the time to like each other before the kissing started. There had been no time for anticipation and even trust to develop between them. There'd been some flirting at that Christmas party, but both of them had been intent on the main event. Abbie's blacking out had probably been some sort of psychological means of self-protection, he thought wryly, because it was a certainty that she didn't make a habit of behaving the way she had that night. Not with a stranger, she didn't.

Was he giving up on Abbie? On their marriage? Cord's eyes narrowed at his own reflection, and then abruptly he finished tossing his personal belongings into his shaving kit.

A short time later Cord drove away from Abbie's house; his car was loaded with his clothes.

After hours of aimless wandering at a shopping mall, Abbie drove home. She pressed the remote and the garage door opened; the garage was empty.

She went inside, to the closet where she had hung Cord's things; there was a two-foot section of vacant rod next to her winter coats. She checked the guest room and noted that Gary had made the bed before leaving. The closet was empty. Both bathrooms contained nothing but damp towels.

Taking a deep breath she peered into the den and the living room, telling herself that she was not going to cry, that this was what she had wanted all along. Attempting to live under the same roof with Cord, even part-time, was absurd. Now he would have more than just his weekends free and could receive his calls from that "Ash" person without embarrassment.

And she, Abbie, could get on with her life.

She fluttered around the kitchen, putting some cups in the dishwasher, wiping counters with the dishcloth, watering the small jade plant sitting on the windowsill above the sink.

Her thoughts were jumping around. There were a dozen important tasks to take care of before September, preparing the nursery, purchasing baby clothes and equipment, choosing names, discussing a maternity leave from her job with Bob Sidwell, a dozen things. And reading. She had been neglecting her reading lately. And certainly the house should be thoroughly cleaned, every room, before the baby was brought home.

Suddenly deflated, Abbie plopped onto the nearest chair. The closest thing she had ever experienced to the emptiness she was feeling now were the days and nights immediately following Nick's funeral. And really there was no comparison, because Cord was too healthy, if anything. So healthy he couldn't sleep in the same bed with a woman without...

Feeling utterly defeated, Abbie put her head down and covered her face with her hands. Cord was gone. Their sham of a marriage was over. They would share no more evening meals. There would be no more conversation between them beyond what Cord thought necessary, if even that. She had no instinct on whether or not he would want to keep track of her prenatal progress. For that matter, she had no instinct on anything Cord might want.

Abbie was still sitting in the same spot when Sherry rapped on the patio door. Rising sluggishly, Abbie got up and unlocked the door. "Come on in."

Sherry stepped inside. "How're you doing, Ab?"

"I'll live."

"You're down in the dumps."

"To say the least. Sit down. Would you like a cold drink or something?"

Sherry pulled out a chair from the table and sat down. "Nothing, thanks. I saw Cord leave. He was only here about an hour after we got back from the airport. Abbie, on the

drive home he talked...only a little...about the two of you.
He said he didn't know how to get through to you."

"He might try ordinary affection," Abbie snapped. "The
only thing Cord understands is..." She clamped her lips
together before she went too far. Wasn't she as much to
blame for their intimacy as Cord was? She could have said
no. He certainly hadn't forced her to make love.

"He took all his things, didn't he?" Sherry questioned
sadly. At Abbie's positive head shake, she sighed. "I
thought so."

Abbie sat down across the table from Sherry. "I don't
know how to get through to him, either, you know. Why did
he tell you how he felt? Did he think you had a bag of magical answers?"

"I got the feeling that he wanted me to tell you how he
felt. I also don't think he expected you to be gone when he
got back."

"I...didn't want to stand around and watch him move
out," Abbie said in a ragged voice. "I went to the Mead-
ows Mall." Nervous, she got up again. "Are you sure you
wouldn't like something to drink? There's some of that fruit
punch left from last night."

"I'll have some if you are."

Abbie went to the refrigerator and opened the door. She
reached for the jar of punch and frowned. "What's this?"
An envelope was taped to the jar. Forgetting the punch, she
brought the envelope to the table. "He left a note in the refrigerator?" Abbie questioned incredulously, sinking to her
chair. The envelope was sealed and she tore it open, mum-
bling, "The man's as mad as a hatter. We both are."

There was more than a note inside. She gaped at the
check. "It's for five thousand dollars!" Quickly she unfolded the single piece of paper.

Dear Abbie,
Use this money for whatever you need for the baby. If
it's not enough, just let me know. If you don't mind,
I'd like to call about once a week.

                                        Cord

Silently, tensely, Abbie reread the note and then passed it to Sherry. She stared at the check again, resentfully. "Does he really think I would take this much money from him? Can't he be reasonable about anything?"

"Abbie," Sherry said gently. "He wants to help."

"Then let him offer a sensible amount! What does he think I'm going to do, build a nursery from the ground up?"

"Abbie, you're angry over nothing. Over a kindness."

Abbie burst into tears. The check fluttered to the floor when she covered her face and moaned, "I know, I know. I haven't done anything right in so long, it's a wonder *anyone's* still talking to me. I drove him away, Sherry. He tried to talk to me and I wouldn't let him. I love him," Abbie wailed. "And he doesn't love me. How could he? I've been so mean and nasty, no man would put up with me for long."

Sherry let her cry for a while, then reached out and patted her hand. "I don't know one single person who would have handled the situation any better. It's been tough for you since the day you found out about the baby. Stop crucifying yourself, and stop crucifying Cord, too. The two of you made some mistakes, but you don't have to pay for them for the rest of your lives." Getting up, Sherry went over to the box of tissues on the counter and returned with a handful. "Here, blow your nose."

Abbie obeyed and ultimately gave her friend a shaky smile. "I can't take that much money from him."

"That's your decision. But call him and tell him what you will take. Don't sit around and stew about it. You're not doing either yourself or the baby any good this way."

Abbie didn't phone Cord, but for some reason she felt a whole lot better about the situation. She took his check to work with her on Monday and put it in the mail along with a note.

Dear Cord,
I appreciate your generosity, but I don't need this much money from you. At this point, I anticipate the costs of

a nursery and equipment to be around two thousand, which you may pay half of, if you wish.

It's all right if you want to call occasionally.

Abbie

During her lunch hours Abbie began making plans to turn the guest room into a nursery. After a few days, though, she decided that she could do without a den much easier than she could a guest room. But she wanted the nursery in the existing guest room, which meant some major changes in the house. Her ambitious project expanded when she decided to recarpet the entire house, rather than just the nursery.

She picked up carpet samples from one dealer, paint and wallpaper swatches from another dealer, then walked around the house and tried to visualize new colors and textures in the various rooms.

The days flew by. On Thursday evening the telephone rang. She picked it up without worrying that the caller might be Cord.

"Hello, Abbie."

Her stomach took a sudden lurch. "Hello, Cord. How are you?"

"Fine. And you?"

"I'm fine."

"Really fine? You're feeling well?"

"I'm feeling very well."

"Good," Cord said quietly. "I've been in L.A. for the last couple of days. Your note was delivered while I was gone. Are you sure about returning the check? It doesn't seem like too much to me."

"Believe me, I won't be spending that kind of money. My insurance is taking care of the medical costs. I've already priced some furniture and other things and I'm really sure that two thousand should cover it."

"And you'll only take half from me."

"That seems fair to me," Abbie said.

"Well, let me know if you need more. In fact, let me know if you need anything." When Abbie didn't answer right away, Cord said, "You won't do that, will you?"

"I'll let you know if I spend more than two thousand, Cord."

"But you won't ask me for anything."

"That's . . . hard to say," Abbie hedged.

"Never mind, you don't have to say it. I know you won't. You're independent to the core, Abbie."

"I've had to be, Cord."

"Yeah, I guess you have. Not that there's anything wrong with independence. Just makes it hard for a man to take care of a woman, when she doesn't need him worrying about her. Well, I'll let you go. Talk to you soon."

"Good night," Abbie murmured. "Thanks for calling."

She puzzled about Cord's final comment while she got ready for bed. He wanted to take care of her? If he did, it was a recent development. He had been more than ready to agree to the independent-finances clause in their prenuptial agreement. Their unusual marital arrangement had forced them into areas that most couples never even thought of, but it only made sense to maintain separate entities when it was all going to end after September. In November, actually. They had agreed to divorce when the baby was two months old.

Cord's Thursday-evening calls became routine. During the second one, he told Abbie that he'd sent Gary the photos taken during their visit. Neither of them mentioned the wedding pictures or referred to their final weekend together. Neither of them mentioned anything personal at all, for that matter, other than the state of Abbie's health. The calls were brief and to the point. *How are you? Do you need anything?*

Meanwhile, Abbie's body was changing. She started wearing maternity clothes. The house was undergoing her planned metamorphosis. She hired two young men from the neighborhood to move furniture around, and painters and wallpaper hangers. Emotionally, Abbie felt unusually stable. Cord came to mind often, but she was in a nesting mode and avoided disturbing thoughts about their inevitable split in November.

Sherry happily announced plans to spend her June vacation in Virginia with Gary. A normal Las Vegas summer was settling in, and the heat bothered Abbie in a way she had never before noticed. She shopped for the baby while Sherry was gone, and by the end of the month everything was as ready for September as Abbie could make it.

July was pure torture. The heat was smothering, and Abbie got up an hour earlier than normal to take her daily walks while there was still a trace of nighttime coolness in the air.

August 14 was her last working day before the onset of her two-month maternity leave. Getting out of the heat seemed imperative, and she rented a condo on a California beach for two weeks. The closest city was San Luis Obispo, and the area was familiar as Abbie had spent several previous vacations near San Luis.

She told Cord where she would be for the next two weeks during his usual Thursday-evening call. "I have the phone number of the condo, if you want it."

"I want it, but are you sure you should be so far away from your doctor right now?"

"The baby isn't due for over a month yet, Cord. I really have to get out of the heat for a while. Dr. Leighton approves, and I'll be back before the first of September."

It struck Abbie that Cord had become little more than a concerned voice on the phone. She could talk to him now without startled emotions. Months had gone by since they had last seen each other, since that awful weekend of bickering and passion, and the peace had been nurturing.

"Well, enjoy yourself," Cord said, and Abbie detected a note of uneasiness in his voice.

"I'll be fine. The baby will be fine," she added, remembering that Cord wouldn't be calling her at all if not for the baby.

It was a relief to quit working. Abbie hadn't gained any excessive weight, but she was definitely noticing the additional poundage around her middle and she tired easily. The women at the station gave her a huge baby shower just prior to the fourteenth, and the men sent gifts. Along with what she had purchased, she had so many beautiful things for the baby, there was barely room in the nursery bureau for everything.

On the fifteenth, Abbie said goodbye to Sherry, locked her house and drove to California. The trip took all day, but she thoroughly enjoyed being out of Vegas and the heat and arrived at the pretty, little condo with fine expectations for the upcoming two weeks.

The time passed in long, lazy walks on the beach, cool ocean breezes and leisurely evenings with a good book. Occasionally she thought of Ron Harrison's elation and his obvious hope that she wouldn't return to work on the scheduled date, but nothing seemed to mar the mellowness of Abbie's mood.

Cord called on Thursday evening, as Abbie anticipated. "So, how's the beachcomber doing?" he questioned lightly.

"Wonderful," Abbie answered honestly. "It's beautiful here...and cool."

"You're feeling well, then."

"I'm feeling like a new woman."

"Abbie, it occurred to me that we never did get around to that portrait session."

Abbie frowned. "But you have to know that was only a ploy to meet you."

Cord chuckled in her ear. "Yes, of course. But I really would like to do your portrait. For the baby's album," he added quickly. "Would you mind?"

"Well...no. But not now, Cord. After the baby's born, okay?" Abbie laughed. "I'm not exactly looking my best these days."

"You couldn't look anything but your best," Cord said softly. "Abbie, I think about you all the time. May I see you when you get home?"

Some of the old tension invaded Abbie's system. She couldn't get back on that disturbing track—not yet, at least. "Cord," she said quietly. "I'd...rather not. We'll see each other when the baby's born. Please don't ask for more right now."

After a silence, Cord said, "You're right. We'll see a lot of each other in another month. Take care, Abbie."

Later, lying in bed with the sound of the surf coming through the window, Abbie felt again the turmoil of too much feeling for Cord. There was a part of her that would forever be in love with him; she would never see him again without enduring a sense of sorrow, of loss.

Abbie sighed. Had any woman anywhere trapped herself into an unnerving situation more efficiently than she had? There would be constant occasions to taunt her, birthdays, holidays, her child's first day of school. Cord would want to take part in everything, the same as she would. Neither of them could do it all; they were going to be faced with an enormous number of decisions. And they had to handle them all tactfully and intelligently so that their child was never hurt by the tension between them.

Every couple had problems to overcome. Take Sherry and Gary, for instance. They were in love—Sherry's vacation in Virginia had cinched that—and now they were faced with the diversity of their careers. Each was successful in his own field, and which of them would or could give up what he had spent his life building to be with the other?

But no one that Abbie knew had the kind of problems she and Cord did. Their relationship had started, apparently, with the impact of a hurricane. Which she only barely remembered. Dammit, *why* did she only barely remember it? She hadn't had *that* much to drink!

On Saturday morning while walking barefoot in the surf, Abbie winced at a strange spasm in her lower back. About a half hour later she felt another one. It was more twinge than pain, but it made her uneasy and she returned to the condo.

By midafternoon she knew that something was wrong and called Dr. Leighton's office in Las Vegas. He called her back an hour later. "Are you having a problem, Abbie?"

She explained the spasms in her lower back, which were becoming alarmingly close together.

"Any spotting?"

"Some, yes."

Dr. Leighton asked several more questions, which Abbie answered. "Sounds like you're in labor, Abbie. Is anyone there with you?"

"No, but I've made friends with one of the neighbors. She's usually home during the day and told me to call any time if I needed any help."

"I think you should have your neighbor drive you to the hospital."

And so, Abbie's son was born in San Luis Obispo. He was an ounce under six pounds and twenty inches long, a beautiful baby boy with a full head of black hair. His time of birth was 4:16 a.m. on August the twenty-second, and because he was a full month premature, he was placed in an incubator.

Exhausted, Abbie slept until a nurse came into her room around seven with a cheerful, "Good morning, Mrs. Durant."

Abbie's first clear thought was that she had to call Cord. While the nurse adjusted the blinds and brought sunshine into the room, Abbie sat up and reached for the telephone on the bedside stand.

"Breakfast will be along in a few minutes," the nurse announced. "Then we'll get you out of that bed for a bath."

Abbie smiled. "Thank you." She dialed Cord's Las Vegas condo number as the nurse left. He answered on the second ring with a sleepy, "Hello."

"Sorry if I woke you, but I'm in the hospital. You have a son. He was..."

Cord came awake fast. "A son! You had the baby? Where? Where are you?"

"In San Luis Obispo. Everything's fine. The baby is being given special attention because he came early, but he's fine, Cord." Abbie proudly recited her son's vital statistics. "And he's got a shock of black hair. He's beautiful, Cord, so beautiful it makes me cry to look at him."

"Then you've seen him? And held him?"

"Yes, I have."

"Oh, Abbie. God, I've got to get there. I'll catch the first plane out. A boy. I wanted a boy, but I couldn't bring myself to say so. A girl would have been great, too, but a boy. Abbie, what about his name?"

"I have several in mind, my father's, for one. If you're really coming, maybe we could make that decision together."

"I'm coming. Nothing short of complete global destruction could keep me from coming. And thanks, Abbie. I'll never forget that you didn't choose his name by yourself."

Tears were clogging Abbie's throat when she put down the phone. Her emotions were very fragile this morning. The birth had not been easy, and she knew that she had to look as wrung out as she felt.

A shower and shampoo helped immensely. Standing, she was much stronger than she had thought she would be. Breakfast had been good and she'd eaten every bite. With some makeup brightening her face and her hair clean and fixed, she felt almost normal. Wearing a robe and slippers, she walked down to the nursery.

The attending nurse let her come in and hold her son for a few moments. It was time for a feeding and Abbie gave him a bottle. The doctor appeared and told her that the baby was strong and healthy, and that he would only require monitoring for a few days, just to make sure, as they took no chances with preemies.

Abbie returned to her room and dozed until lunch was delivered. She was still eating when Cord walked in.

They looked at each other. Abbie's senses went flying. He was crisply clean and so handsome she could barely breathe.

"Hi," she finally managed.

Cord moved closer to Abbie's chair. "You look great. How're you feeling?"

"Surprisingly well."

"Did you have a bad time?"

Abbie smiled. "It wasn't so bad." Already, she realized, the trauma of childbirth was dissipating. "Have you seen him?"

"I came here first."

Abbie's heart skipped a beat. She couldn't have imagined him seeing her before his son.

"Go and see him, Cord. The nursery is just down the hall to the right. Tell the nurse who you are and she'll let you hold him."

"I'll be right back," Cord promised.

"There's no hurry. I'm not going anywhere," Abbie said with a small laugh. Alone in the room again, she sighed and laid her head back, thinking, *And so it begins.*

Her lunch tray had been taken away when Cord returned. Abbie stood by the window. "Should you be out of bed?"

She laughed. "I'm leaving the hospital in the morning, Cord. I'm perfectly all right."

"The baby's leaving with you?"

"No. The doctor wants him monitored for a few more days."

"But he's all right, isn't he?" Cord asked anxiously. "He's so tiny."

"He came a month early, and they watch preemies until they're certain."

"Then they're not certain at this point?"

"The doctor is only being cautious, Cord." Abbie regarded him with a steady gaze. "What do you think of him?"

"He's unbelievable. I didn't expect him to be so small. I held him in my two hands, Abbie. His eyes opened and I swear he was looking right at me. And all that hair. He's beautiful, Abbie, the most beautiful thing I've ever seen."

A soft sigh rippled through Abbie. Holding out a vague hope of Cord feeling no more than mild affection for his son had been for naught: he was as smitten by that tiny life in the nursery as she was.

Abbie returned to the chair and sat down. "You're going home tomorrow?" Cord questioned.

"To the condo I rented here, yes."

"And then?"

"Well . . . I really haven't made any definite plans. I have another week at the condo so I'll stay there until the baby's released. I guess I can use a few days' rest. I feel good, but it's a long drive back to Vegas."

"So you plan on driving back to Vegas with the baby, when the doctor releases him?"

"Do you have a problem with that?" Abbie asked.

"Well, hell, it's a long drive, Abbie. Anything could happen. You'll be all alone on the highway with a newborn baby."

Abbie frowned. He did have a point. She loved her son on sight—maybe even before that; but she wasn't used to factoring a baby into her plans yet. "What are you getting at?"

"A flight back to Vegas. I can arrange to have your car brought home, and you and the baby will be safely back in your own house in a few hours."

"All right." Abbie nodded. She couldn't tell if she was simply too tired to argue with Cord or if, for once, she didn't want to.

# Twelve

---

**They** named their son Jason Elliot, after both their fathers. Five days after Jason Elliot Durant's birth, mother and son flew from San Luis Obispo to Las Vegas. Cord, with the same ease of efficiency he had shown planning their wedding, had taken care of every detail for Abbie. His appointment schedule would not permit him to stay in the San Luis area, but when Abbie and son deplaned at McCarran International in Las Vegas, Cord was there to meet them.

"Well, I'll be darned," Cord exclaimed softly when Abbie peeled back the lightweight blanket so he could see his son's face. "He's already grown some."

"He's over six pounds now," Abbie said proudly.

"I've got a hired limo waiting with the motor running," Cord told her. "It's hotter than Hades outside and I didn't want the two of you getting into a sweltering car."

"That's very thoughtful."

He grinned. "I'm a thoughtful guy."

He was teasing, Abbie knew, but he was also sexy, handsome, the father of her baby and her husband, and all of those qualities seemed to be as blatant as if they were written in red ink across his forehead. Walking through the airport, Abbie was aware that the three of them looked like a close family unit. She carried Jason, but Cord held onto her arm, as any protective and loving husband and father might do in a public place.

She was in love with him, Abbie thought with some sadness. Obviously he was here because of his son, but it felt wonderfully fulfilling to be met at the airport and fussed over.

There was only a few seconds' exposure to the heat, when they exited the terminal and walked to the limo at the curb. Its cool interior was heavenly, and Abbie sank back onto the plush seat with a sigh of pleasure. She loosened Jason's blanket, and for the first five minutes of the ride home, Cord did little more than stare at his son.

"I'm afraid of him," he finally said with some awe. "Is he as breakable as he looks?"

Abbie laughed. "Not at all. You just have to be careful to hold his head."

"Well, I sure won't be driving off with him for a while, I don't mind telling you."

At the reminder of their formal agreement, Abbie's smile faltered. Whatever feelings she had for Cord, his were focused on Jason, which she would be wise to remember. "I'm glad you see the sensibility of leaving him in my care."

"Who's going to take care of him when you go back to work?"

"I've lined up a highly recommended child-care center that specializes in infant care."

"Strangers?" Cord asked, aghast.

"I *have* to work, Cord," Abbie said defensively.

They stopped talking.

The limo pulled into Abbie's driveway, and the driver hurried to open the door for his passengers. Cord passed the man a bill and a word of thanks, then followed Abbie into the house while the driver unloaded Abbie's luggage. "I parked my car in the garage. Hope you don't mind."

"I don't mind," Abbie replied. "I'm going to bring Jason to the nursery. Would you like to see it?"

"Hey," Cord exclaimed as they started through the house. "What've you done? It looks different."

"It is different, the carpeting, at least. The guest room is where the den was, and the old guest room is now the nursery."

Abbie gently laid her sleeping son in his crib. From behind her Cord said, "Everything looks great, but you didn't do all of this for only two thousand bucks, Abbie."

She glanced back. "I certainly don't expect you to pay for recarpeting my house." She left the crib. "He's sound asleep. Let's leave him alone."

Cord's take-charge tendencies were on full throttle, Abbie realized when he started talking about the dangers and disadvantages of strangers taking care of their baby the second they were away from the nursery.

"I have no other choice," Abbie said with the first noticeable vexation she had felt with Cord in months. "My career is really none of your business, and your disapproval isn't going to change one single thing. I'd appreciate it if you would keep it to yourself."

Cord cocked an eyebrow. "It isn't going to bother you to leave Jason with strangers?"

"Of course it's going to bother me! But it's nearly two months away and I'm going to have to live with it. So are you."

"What about hiring a nanny?"

"I can't afford a nanny."

"But I can."

Abbie swallowed uneasily as a new and disturbing thought arose. Cord apparently could afford a lot of things that were beyond her financial reach, and was their every disagreement on Jason's upbringing going to be decided by the size of their bank accounts?

"We'll talk about it later," Abbie said adamantly.

"Not too much later, I hope."

"Cord, I'm tired. Let's break this up."

"You want me to leave."

"Frankly, yes."

"When may I come back? I'd like to see him often, Abbie."

She sighed wearily. "Come back whenever you feel like it. But please don't give me orders and start finding fault with everything I'm doing."

"Finding fault! Abbie, I trust you implicitly with my son."

"He's my son, too, Cord, or have you already forgotten which one of us gave birth five days ago?"

Cord settled down after a few days, and so did Abbie. There was no question about which of them was more responsible for Jason's care. Cord lovingly held his son and he wasn't afraid of a soiled diaper, but there was much about infant care that perplexed him and he was content to leave schedules and decisions to Abbie.

All the same, he was a whiz with a camera, and he used up countless rolls of film photographing Jason awake, Jason asleep, Jason eating, crying, smiling, waving his arms, spitting and doing everything else that a newborn did by instinct.

It came to Abbie one day without warning that there was really no valid reason for the two of them to wait until November to file for divorce. She froze while a terrible chill went up her spine, and yet it only made sense. They were getting along as well as they ever had and the divorce would be amicable. She was resigned to his presence in her life, and in Jason's, and where else would they go from here but to the conclusion of their agreement?

Tears clouded Abbie's eyes. At odd moments she had been catching Cord's gaze on her with a strangely speculative expression, but he never once got near anything personal between them. Since their infamous wedding day they had disagreed, argued, debated, made love and even held a few civil conversations. They had one area of common ground: Jason. There would never be anything else.

She said nothing to Cord about divorce; he said nothing to her about divorce. On the third of October, when Jason was about six weeks old and Abbie had only two weeks left of her maternity leave, Cord announced a business trip to New York City. He was on his way out after spending an hour in the nursery with his son and he stopped at Abbie's front door with a laugh. "You know, we still haven't done your portrait."

"There's plenty of time," Abbie said quietly.

"Yeah, guess there is. Anyway, Abbie, while I'm gone, expect a surprise."

"What kind of surprise?"

"Don't sound so suspicious. It's a little bizarre, but nothing bad." Cord stepped out onto the front stoop, shoved his hands into the back pockets of his jeans and grinned. "At least *I* don't think it's bad. Maybe you won't either. I'm hoping you won't. Bye, little mother." He leaned over and kissed her square on the mouth, which startled Abbie so much she backed up.

A minute later when Cord was sauntering to his car at the curb, she cursed herself for reacting so negatively to a very nice gesture. He certainly hadn't meant anything suggestive by such an innocuous kiss, and she hadn't had to act like he was attacking her.

"Will either of us ever do anything right?" she whispered as Cord's car pulled away from the curb. Sighing, she went in and closed the door.


That very afternoon a florist delivered a dozen long-stemmed white roses. The card was signed, *A secret admirer.* At first the Victorian phrase made Abbie laugh, but in the next instant she realized that she really had no idea who had sent the flowers. Cord certainly wouldn't sign the card in such an inane fashion, although he had mentioned a surprise. Were these gorgeous roses it?

But roses weren't bizarre, were they?

The next day another delivery truck arrived. Abbie placed the red roses next to the white ones on the coffee table and read the card. *Flowers preach to us if we will hear.* Abbie frowned. The line was lovely and vaguely familiar, from a Christina Rossetti poem, she was fairly certain.

She sat down. Who was doing this? If it was Cord, why wouldn't he sign his name?

At seven that evening the telephone rang. Cord's voice said, "Hello, Abbie. We haven't been formally introduced, but my name is Cord Durant and I'm a big fan of KSTV's six o'clock news."

Abbie pulled the phone away and looked at it as if it had suddenly sprouted horns. Then she brought it back to her ear. "Cord?"

"Yes, Cord Durant. You may have heard of me, as I do have a modest reputation in the field of portrait photography."

"What's wrong with you?" she questioned tartly.

"A few things, nothing major," Cord replied smoothly. "Which I'm hoping you'll agree to discovering for yourself. I'm out of town at present, but I'll be back in Vegas on Friday. I'd be honored if you would have dinner with me."

What on earth was he doing? Why was he speaking as though this was their first conversation? Had he finally lost it completely?

"Cord..."

"I know this must seem presumptuous, me being a total stranger and all, but I've admired you on TV for a long time, and if a man doesn't let a woman know he's interested, they never will get together, will they?"

Abbie's knees gave out and she flopped onto the nearest chair. "I...suppose you have a point," she said hoarsely.

"I understand you have a son."

"A...very beautiful son," she whispered.

"And is he well and happy?"

"Yes. Very. Cord..."

"I happen to know your address. Purely by accident, of course. What time should I pick you up on Friday? Seven? Eight?"

"Uh...sounds fine..." Abbie could barely think. Why was Cord doing this? What in God's name was going on with him? "Cord, did you send me flowers? Roses?"

"Yes, I did. Do you like them?"

"That's not..."

"What's your opinion of courtship, Abbie?"

"Courtship?" she quavered.

"Yes, courtship. You know, when a man courts a woman because he thinks she's beautiful and intelligent and he wants her to know how he feels?"

"Oh, *that* courtship. Well, it seems to be rather...rare these days," Abbie said lamely, although she was beginning to grasp Cord's intentions. Her heart beat faster at her own incredulous thoughts. Was he truly planning to court her? Like an ordinary unmarried man did with an ordinary unmarried woman? He had certainly pegged her surprise right on the money when he'd labeled it "bizarre."

"Too rare," Cord quietly agreed. "I'd like to alter that statistic by two, Abbie. I think you and I have the qualities to do so."

"Time will tell," Abbie whispered.

"Good night, Abbie. I'll see you at seven on Friday evening."

"Good night, Cord." She put the phone down in a daze. A date. He'd called from New York to ask for a date! And he apparently wanted them to start at square one. She got up and paced, not knowing whether to laugh or cry.

Sherry ecstatically agreed to stay with Jason on Friday evening. Abbie began getting ready in mid-afternoon, fretting about what to wear as if Cord hadn't already seen everything in her closet. Her waistline had gone down enormously, but it had a few more inches to go to reach normal, so she began eliminating dresses by fit.

Ultimately she decided on a deep red silk dress with a matching jacket. She fixed her hair and did her makeup with more care than she had taken in months. Her accessories—pumps, jewelry and handbag—were perfect complements to the dress. She was ready and waiting when Sherry came in at quarter to seven.

"You look fantastic, Ab." Because Abbie couldn't seem to stand still, Sherry added, "Settle down, honey. This is the night you've been hoping for."

"I don't really understand what he's doing."

"Sure you do. He wants the same thing you do, only Cord being Cord, he is going at it a little differently. It's romantic, Abbie. Make the most of it."

Abbie was still giving Sherry information on Jason's schedule when the front doorbell rang. Abbie's eyes widened. "He rang the doorbell when he usually just walks in?"

"Are you going to keep him standing out there? Go open the door and let him in," Sherry said with mock acerbity.

The walk through the house to the front door filled Abbie with so much anxious excitement, she wondered if she weren't going to hyperventilate. She opened the door and there was Cord, gorgeous in a dark suit and white shirt with a striking silk tie. His clothing wasn't quite tuxedo formal, but it was close.

"Good evening, Abbie."

She cleared her throat. "Good evening."

"You're even more beautiful in person than you are on television. I suspected that might be the case."

Abbie blushed as his gaze moved down to her shoes and back up to her face, and then she smiled embarrassedly because she was blushing. "Thank you. Come in."

In the living room, she nervously asked, "Would you like something to drink?"

Cord smiled, and his expression contained the remoteness of a stranger and the familiarity of a lover, bedazzling Abbie. "Our reservation is for eight. What I would really like is to take a peek at your son before we leave. Would you mind?"

"No, of course not. He's asleep in the nursery."

Sherry had been staying discreetly out of sight in the nursery, and she grinned broadly when Cord and Abbie walked in. "Hi," she directed to Cord.

"Hello," he said formally. "I don't think we've met. I'm Cord Durant."

Sherry giggled. "And I'm Sherry Newman, Abbie's next-door neighbor."

"I believe you know my brother," Cord said with a perfectly straight face.

Sherry giggled again. "As a matter of fact, I do."

"And this is Jason," Cord said softly while advancing on the crib. The baby slept on his stomach, and Cord laid his hand on his son's diapered bottom for a moment so tender Abbie felt tears threatening her mascara.

"I'll be in the other room," Sherry whispered to Abbie.

Cord turned from the crib with an emotional smile. "He's the most beautiful child I've ever seen. Shall we go?"

"I'll get my purse," Abbie mumbled around the clog in her throat. She managed an unsteady but private word with Sherry before leaving the house. "Is he crazy, or what?"

"He's wonderful, not crazy. Go along with it, Abbie," was Sherry's advice.

Outside, Cord assisted Abbie into his car. When he was behind the wheel he said graciously, "Our reservation is at Rudolph's. Does that suit you?"

"Marvelous choice," Abbie mumbled. Rudolph's was one of the city's more elegant restaurants, which accounted for Cord's formal attire. Her own outfit, thank goodness, was adequate, although sequins were the "in" thing this year.

They made small talk during the drive, mentioning the traffic and the weather, as if they were truly first-time acquaintances. It amazed Abbie that Cord could manage the pretense so well, until she remembered Gary's visit.

At Rudolph's they were seated at once. Cord ordered a bottle of champagne and then dinner. The service was impeccable and the food, when it was delivered, was delicious. Abbie began to relax. Cord talked about his New York trip, reciting several incidents of travel that made her laugh.

The whole charade was amusing but not funny. Behind Cord's commanding facade was something so serious, Abbie was afraid to draw conclusions, rather, instead, relying on questions. Was he hoping to maintain their marriage? Why would he choose this route over a forthright discussion? Did he think that their relationship would be aided by a touch of the comical?

She drank several glasses of champagne with dinner, although Cord abstained after the first glass, reminding Abbie with a smile that he was driving.

They lingered over coffee and dessert, the most heavenly strawberry mousse Abbie had ever put in her mouth, and casually discussed Nevada politics. It was hardly a romantic topic, but with Cord looking at her as if she were the most fabulously beautiful woman in his world, Abbie marveled that her heart didn't explode in her chest.

On the way out, Cord's hand rested against the small of her back, burning her skin beneath her silk jacket and dress. While they waited for the valet to bring the car, he murmured, "We'll have to do this again very soon."

She merely nodded, because she was dizzy and wondering if her spinning head was a result of the champagne or Cord's incredible attentiveness. Tonight he was the man of her dreams, the man of *any* woman's dreams, focused entirely on her, handsome, bright, suave.

He helped her into the car, and wherever he touched her, only what was necessary, became alive and throbbing. The lights of the city blurred for Abbie as Cord maneuvered the car through traffic.

"Do you have to be home at any specific time?" he asked.

"I told Sherry I wouldn't be late," Abbie replied. "She has a meeting in the morning."

"She works on Saturday?"

"Often, yes. She's very dedicated to her career."

"So is Gary. Seems like a major hurdle to anything permanent for them, doesn't it?"

"Every couple has hurdles to overcome."

"Some more formidable than others," Cord agreed quietly. "Do you have time for a drive out to the lake?"

Abbie checked the dash clock and saw that it wasn't quite ten-thirty. "As long as I'm home before midnight."

Friday-night traffic abated with the city lights; the farther they got from the bustle of town, the darker became the night. The car motor was a soothing purr. Cord sent Abbie a smile. "Peaceful, isn't it?"

"Very," she agreed and then tried to remember if she had ever before felt at peace in Cord's presence. Not that she wasn't keenly aware of him, but the sharp edges of their relationship seemed to have been softened by the pleasant evening.

"I've enjoyed tonight, Cord."

"So have I, Abbie. Very much."

The road to Lake Mead was familiar to Abbie. There were clusters of lights along the way, mostly set back from the road. One area, she knew from daylight tours she'd taken, was especially lovely. Splendid homes situated on barren, craggy slopes that gradually dropped to the lake, providing magnificent views for the homeowners.

Abbie looked to Cord for an explanation when he made a left turn from the highway onto a road leading to that particular group of homes.

He merely said, "I want to show you something."

There were large spaces of vacant land between the houses, in some cases because the terrain was too rugged for construction. But some of the land had been leveled into construction lots, and it was onto one of those spacious lots that Cord drove and stopped the car.

"What do you think of the view?" he questioned as he turned off the motor.

The lake was visible only by moonlight and distant dock lights, but as limited as the view was by darkness, it was still breathtaking. "It's beautiful," Abbie murmured. The silence struck her. "And it's so quiet out here." She settled deeper into the seat. "Maybe the owner of this land objects to strangers driving on it."

"I'm the owner, Abbie."

"Oh." Abbie was still enthralled with the lake view, but she turned her head and tried to see Cord in the dark. "Was this what you wanted to show me?"

"I'm thinking of building a house here. What's your opinion? Think living out here is a good idea?"

"Well . . . yes."

"Be a great place to raise kids, don't you think? Clean air, very little traffic? They would go to school in Boulder City. I've always liked Boulder City, haven't you?"

"Boulder City is hard *not* to like, Cord." The small town was born when Hoover Dam was constructed, and it had a quaint charm and rigid laws against gambling. Property values were high, Abbie knew from a news report she had done on the unique little town only the previous spring. Cord had to have paid a small fortune for this lot and view.

"Abbie..." He turned in the seat to face her. "I'm going to tell you what I had in mind when I called from New York."

Abbie sensed that the charade was over and said quietly, "I wish you would."

"We never had any of this, Abbie, a normal dinner date, a movie together, none of the quality time that other couples put in on a relationship. It started bothering me when Gary was here. You know what I'm talking about, the way he and Sherry talked and laughed together. They flirted, Abbie. They teased and played and cut up like a couple of kids. That's what it's all about, Abbie. That's how two people learn to like each other, and it's what we never did.

"Anyway, I got to thinking that maybe it wasn't too late. I knew it was silly to call and pretend we hadn't yet met, but it was in my mind to court you for at least a month. Take you to dinner, to movies, to ball games, and to keep my hands to myself. Give you a chance to like me."

Abbie nearly said that she *did* like him, that she loved him, but declaring any such feelings seemed premature. For one thing, she understood what he was saying, perfectly. There hadn't been one dram of honest "liking" between them, not from her, not from him.

"Abbie, I don't want to keep my hands off of you for another month, but I'll do it if it will help our relationship. If you like this courtship idea, we'll do it. It's up to you. You have to be honest with me about it. Like you told me once, I'm not a mind reader."

Abbie didn't need three days to think about it. "I like it Cord. I like it very much. Tonight was...special."

"You realize that I'm thinking of voiding that damned agreement. For Jason, of course, but for us, as well. Abbie, there's something very powerful between us. I don't believe I'm the only one who feels it."

Abbie's pulse had quickened about five minutes before, and now it took another sudden jump in speed. "I've...felt it all along," she admitted, her voice unsteady. "Why else would I have...?"

"Made love with me?" Cord said softly. "How I want you. Do you have any idea how much? How I ache when I see you holding our son?" He stirred, inadvertently sending a drift of his after-shave in Abbie's direction, which nearly undid her. He was gorgeous, he was sexy, and he was attempting to make plans for a permanently united future.

Maybe *she* was the one who didn't want to keep her hands to herself, Abbie thought when a tide of desire nearly choked her. Couldn't they make their decision right now? If they both gave everything, if they talked about feelings without any reservations, would they have to wait a month to be truly together?

She could sense his desire and his rigid determination to control it. The silky night seemed wrapped around the two of them. She wanted to be in his arms. With this new understanding between them, torturing themselves for weeks wasn't logical.

"Cord," she whispered while sliding across the seat. He seemed startled, but lifted his arms to welcome her, and the contact of their bodies was like an electrical shock for Abbie. She raised her face and pressed her lips to his throat. "Your plan worked beautifully, but I think it's a little unrealistic to think we can wait so long before taking what we both want so much."

"Abbie, are you sure?"

She felt the tremble in his arms, the heat that radiated through his clothing. She felt liquid and glowing from her own heat. "I'm sure," she breathlessly whispered.

Their mouths searched and mated in the darkness. Cord's hand was immediately under Abbie's jacket and on her breasts. Their first kiss evolved to another of intense urgency. The night quiet was shattered by raspy breathing and the rustling of clothing as they strained together.

There was no restraint in their embrace, no ruffled emotions or nagging reluctance. They were coming together as true and certain lovers, needing each other with a desperation born of longtime abstinence.

"Let's go home," Abbie whispered raggedly.

"Yes," Cord agreed tersely. He took one last, lingering kiss and then untangled himself from her arms to start the car.

She rode with her head on his shoulder and stars in her eyes.

# Thirteen

---

"**I**'m going to stop at the condo to pick up a few things," Cord said, placing a tender kiss on Abbie's forehead while keeping his eyes on the road.

She snuggled closer and sighed dreamily. "I'll wait in the car."

"It's close to midnight, honey. I think you'd better come in with me. We'll only be a minute."

Feeling as soft and malleable as a piece of clay, Abbie allowed Cord to steer her from the car and into his building. They kissed in the elevator, with Cord leaning against the wall and Abbie leaning into him. The ride to the fifth floor was much too short for her.

Inside the condo, Abbie sank onto a living-room chair while Cord went to his bedroom. Her mind was awhirl with kisses and caresses, and with what was to come when they got to her house.

Her gaze absently swept the room, and abruptly she sat up straighter: Cord's Christmas tree had been in that corner. She remembered the tree and that they had made love on the carpet. Why couldn't she remember it all?

Cord came through the bedroom door with a small bag, announcing that he was all set.

Arm in arm they returned to the elevator and ultimately Cord's car. When they arrived at Abbie's house, Sherry greeted them with the announcement that Jason had followed his schedule like a little angel.

"I'll see Sherry home," Cord said softly to Abbie. "Won't be but a minute."

"I'll be waiting," she told him with a hundred ardent promises in her eyes.

Alone, she checked on Jason, who was sleeping like a lamb, then hurried across the hall to her bedroom and turned on one lamp. Bypassing a nightgown, she quickly undressed and got into bed, and then lay there with a chokingly excited heartbeat. Her entire body was throbbing, and there wasn't a sensible thought in her head beyond her already ingrained habit of listening for Jason.

She heard Cord coming into the house and then his footsteps, muffled by her new plush carpeting. He stopped in the bedroom doorway to absorb the arousing sight of Abbie waiting for him, then went on in and began removing his own clothes.

Nude, he climbed into bed and lay within the inviting cradle of Abbie's thighs. It was as if there had been no interruption between their first kiss in the car and these. She moved seductively beneath him, touching him in a beguilingly intimate manner. "Tonight is like our first time together was," he whispered against her lips. "You've bewitched me, Abbie."

"I'm glad. Hold me, Cord. Love me."

"I am, baby. I will." He kissed the tender underside of her jaw and then her breasts, taking their sweet crests into his mouth. Moaning, Abbie held his head to her chest, entrancing him with her unbridled passion. He savored her taste and felt her deep inside himself.

Making love with Cord was an emotional storm for Abbie. Their personal turbulences seemed to create vibrations in the very air they were breathing. The bedding whispered against bare skin as it was brushed aside. Neither hinted at slowing down for protection; it was, Cord thought again, exactly as that night in December.

Abbie awoke to inquisitive hands on her body, moving slowly, coaxing her into a dreamy world of sensual pleasure. They made love while still half-asleep, wordlessly, as naturally as if they had never shared one moment of dissension.

At two she awoke again and crawled sleepily out of bed to tend Jason. When her precious son was fed, dry and sleeping again, she returned to her bed and realized that Cord hadn't even heard his son's demanding wails. Smiling indulgently, she snuggled close and Cord's arms came around her.

Jason sounded another alarm at six. Abbie opened her eyes to an empty room. Cord's dress shirt was draped over a chair, but his suit was hanging in the closet. She got out of bed, slipped into a robe and hurried to the nursery. Her hair was in her eyes and she pushed it back before reaching into the crib to pick up her son with a soothing, "There, there, little darling. Mommy's here."

She was sitting in the living room with the baby consuming his six o'clock bottle when Cord strolled in. He was wearing his running shorts and shoes, and his skin glistened with perspiration.

He dropped a kiss on Abbie's lips, "Morning, sweetheart," and touched Jason's hand. The baby's tiny fingers closed around his father's forefinger. "Morning, big guy."

Abbie smiled. "You were out early."

"Couldn't sleep once the sun was up." His eyes probed hers. "How're you doing this morning?"

"I could use a shower. Mind holding your son while he finishes his bottle?"

Cord grinned and reached for the baby. "Come to Papa, big guy."

"I'll hurry," Abbie promised.

"Thanks. I need a shower, too."

Abbie wrinkled her nose at him. "Thought I smelled something."

Cord laughed. "Can't help sweating when I run, sweetheart."

Bending over, Abbie kissed his lips and looked into his eyes. "I like it. I like everything about you this morning."

"Wait till Jason's through eating and we'll take that shower together," Cord said with a sexy grin.

"But after his bottle comes his bath. Sorry, big guy," Abbie said with a teasing flip of the lock of hair on Cord's forehead.

Ten minutes later she returned to the living room, refreshed and feeling as bright as a new penny. Jason was asleep and Cord was gazing down at his son with the most adoring look Abbie had ever seen on anyone's face. She sat beside them on the sofa. "He's kind of special, isn't he?"

"Abbie, I can't tell you what he means to me."

"I feel the same."

"I know you do. Abbie, we've got to straighten out our lives."

"Agreed," she said softly.

"I've been thinking. I'm going to build that house I mentioned last night. It'll be great for the three of us."

"Well...I can't deny that the idea of building a new house is exciting," Abbie admitted, feeling warm all over from the rapport between them.

"We also have to talk about your job, Abbie."

A small cloud slipped through Abbie's happiness. "What about my job, Cord?"

"Heck, you certainly don't have to hold down a full-time job anymore."

Abbie's smile slipped a little more. "But what if I *want* my job, Cord? I happen to love what I do, and I worked very hard to get where I am."

"If it's a matter of money..."

"It's not. Oh, I've had to earn a living, make no mistake." Abbie got up. "Cord, it's not about money. I feel very good about my career, and I'd like to stay with it for as long as the station owners are satisfied with my work. Don't ask me to give it up."

"Jason needs his mother," Cord said with some coolness.

"He needs his father, too, but needing his parents doesn't mean they can't have a life beyond the four walls of his nursery. Let's put the shoe on the other foot. Would *you* be willing to give up your studios to tend our son?"

"That's different, Abbie, and you know it is."

"No, I'm afraid I don't." Jason was sound asleep on his father's lap, and Abbie decided that it wouldn't do any harm to delay his bath for one morning. "Let me bring him to his room," she said quietly. "We need to talk about this, Cord."

Cord passed the sleeping infant to Abbie, and when mother and son had left the room he stretched his legs out from the sofa and scowled at his running shoes. Getting Abbie to agree to anything without a battle was damned near impossible. Why should she work? The Durants had never been penniless to begin with, and he made more than enough money to take care of his family. For that matter, he probably earned more in two months than Abbie's annual income.

Abbie slipped back into the living room and chose a chair instead of the sofa. She and Cord exchanged a long look.

"Is my career going to be a major problem?" she finally asked, keeping emotion out of her voice.

"I hope not."

He was mule stubborn, which she'd known from that first day in his studio. Abbie's own pulse rate felt erratic to her. This was a crucial discussion. They had made enormous strides last night, but there was still a fragility to their relationship that didn't exactly bolster her confidence.

"Cord," she said with studied calmness. "Do you realize that you've never told me you loved me?"

His expression changed from balky to startled. "That's not true."

"Oh? You mean that you've said it and I didn't hear it? If that's the case, I apologize."

"Dammit, Abbie, I *must* have said it." His eyes narrowed. "I don't recall you saying it either."

"I haven't," Abbie admitted. "But I do. I've been in love with you for a long time."

"How long?"

"Long enough that I thought about telling you before Gary's visit."

"But you didn't do it. Why not?"

"Because I felt nothing from you except dedicated concern for your unborn child. In some ways that's still the most dominant emotion I'm able to pick up from you."

Cord's face flushed. "After last night you can say that?"

"Last night was wonderful. You said it was like our night together in December. I wish I could remember all of it, but since I can't, I'll take your word for it."

Cord leaned forward. "Abbie, you have to know how I feel about you. Why would I go to so much trouble to seal our marriage if I didn't love you? I fell hard that first night. I thought you did, too. Your memory lapse was a blow I hadn't seen coming, and when you finally called the studio and asked to see me, my hopes hit the ceiling. Your attitude..."

"Cord, I was running scared. My job..."

"Yes, your job," he interjected gruffly. "Your job's the only reason you came to me."

"Not the only reason," Abbie objected. "But I can't deny how upset I was over the prospect of facing my employers." She stopped for a breath. "We seem to be laying our cards on the table, don't we? Cord, do you remember our initial interaction as peaceable? As generous? You issued ultimatums one right after the other so fast I didn't have time to absorb their implications. I berated myself after our hurry-up wedding, because I was terribly uncertain about having made the right decision."

Cord's frown was so deep, his eyes looked like slits. His voice came out low and tense. "And yet you fell in love with me. I couldn't have been as bad as you're making me out to be now, not if you fell in love, Abbie."

"Every truth between us sounds like an accusation," Abbie said in a near whisper. "That's not my intention."

"I love you. Is that truth enough for you?"

Abbie blinked at the sudden moisture in her eyes. "No, Cord, it isn't. You're still issuing ultimatums."

"I've been offering suggestions on our future, Abbie, suggestions that make a lot of sense, not issuing ultimatums!"

"I'm sorry you see it that way." Abbie stood up. "I'm not going to quit working, Cord. And Jason won't be neglected by it, either. This is one disagreement you're not going to win." She retired to the kitchen, where she put on a pot of coffee and tried desperately to steady the trembling of her hands and legs.

She was aware of the master-bathroom shower running. The coffee was finished before Cord appeared, showered, shaved and wearing faded jeans and a white polo shirt, and when he walked into the kitchen Abbie was sitting at the table with a cup in front of her.

"I'm going to the studio," he said without explanation. "I'll see you later."

"Wouldn't you like some breakfast before you go?" The quivering sensation in her system was like a death knell.

"Thanks, but I'm not hungry. See you later."

Abbie watched him go with a heavy heart. They'd gotten so close to the finish line. Could she really let him walk out of her life rather than do what he asked? Never mind that his request seemed contrary and unreasonable, could she allow their relationship to permanently disintegrate when their goals were primarily the same?

She loved him, she would always love him, but did he love her in the same intensely eternal way?

The studio was vacant. Cord walked into the cavernous, echoing building and locked the door behind him to forestall any drop-in callers. He needed to be alone.

After putting on a pot of coffee to brew, he wandered the large working area of his professional quarters, stopping at the wall of photos without seeing any of them. Abbie was tearing a hole in his gut. Why, when everything else was perfect, would she balk at quitting a job she no longer needed?

He wanted her home with Jason. His working hours were erratic, which she well knew from their stab at part-time cohabitation in the early months of their marriage. Her suggestion that *he* give up his career to tend their son was ludicrous. Where did the woman get such screwy notions?

Was he wrong? Was Abbie? Frowning, Cord poured himself a cup of coffee and sat at his desk to drink it. After a few minutes of stewing, he picked up the phone and called the one person who had always been there with moral support when he needed it.

"Gary, hi," he said, grateful that his brother had answered.

"Cord! Hey, I was just thinking about you. How's everything in Vegas?"

"Not so good. Abbie and I are at an impasse on a particularly sore subject and I guess I need to hear someone tell me I'm not wrong."

"Are you wrong, Cord?"

"*You* tell me, Gary. I want Abbie to quit her job and stay home with Jason. Does that sound unreasonable to you?"

"How is the little guy?"

"Fantastic, incredible, unbelievable."

Gary chuckled. "What else could he be, being your son and my nephew? Be sure and send me some more pictures."

"I'll keep them coming, don't worry. But what's your opinion of Abbie quitting?"

"Seems to me that it should be her decision, Cord. Sorry if that's not what you wanted to hear, but Abbie's got her head on straight. I trust her to do what's right, don't you? Deep down?"

Deep down Cord wasn't feeling so good. He'd always gone to Gary with his problems. In fact, keeping the true nature of his marriage from his older brother was the only time he'd ever strayed from a pattern that had started when he was thirteen and suddenly without parents.

It was startling to hear Gary talk about trusting Abbie when he never had. He hadn't even thought about trust between them, because he'd been so positive from the inception of their relationship that he was right. Not that he'd been wrong to persist in the pursuit of his child, but he might have handled the situation with a little more wisdom.

The past ten months flicked through his mind, events, discussions, arguments, demands. He loved Abbie and had never really stressed that fact.

"I hope you two aren't having a serious problem," Gary said in his ear.

"It could be serious, if we let it get that far. I'm calling from the studio. I think I'll sign off and go home, Gary. I owe Abbie an apology, and the sooner it's said, the better."

This wasn't about Abbie's job, Cord realized when he walked into the house and went looking for her. Arguing over her job was merely a symptom of a much deadlier disease, which he was determined to cure once and for all. He found her in the master bedroom making the bed. When he had left the house her hair was still wet from her shower. Now it was dry and fixed and she was wearing makeup and a satiny pale green robe that came to her knees.

He stopped in the doorway. Abbie straightened up from the bed. "Hi."

"Hi. Busy?"

"Nothing that can't wait." If her heart were big and obvious and vulnerable in her eyes, Abbie didn't care. "Cord, if you really want me to quit my job, I'll do it."

An enormous sorrow brought tears to Cord's eyes. He blinked them away, but not before Abbie saw them. She came around the foot of the bed. "You're feeling bad. I'm sorry."

He rushed forward and crushed her into a fierce embrace, burying his face in her hair. "You've done nothing to be sorry for. I've got so many things to apologize for, I don't know where to begin."

Abbie's arms squeezed tighter around his waist. "Oh, Cord. I can't let anything come between us, not ever again. What's important to you is important to me. I'll talk to Bob Sidwell right away and..."

"*No!*" Cord pushed her away enough to see her face. "You'll quit only if *you* want to. I'll never mention it again.'' His eyes were dark and liquid with emotion. ''Abbie, I love you more than anything else in the world. I know now why I couldn't tell Gary about that miserable damned agreement. It was because I never believed it. Deep down I was certain that I could keep you. I've loved you from the first moment I set eyes on you at that party. I manipulated you, and forced you to marry me with threats. I feel like a fool, because I know now that a little kindness and trust would have brought us together a whole lot quicker.''

Tears were dripping down Abbie's cheeks. ''I have regrets, too, Cord. I'm not proud of how I fought your every suggestion. I wasn't a very nice person, and I wish I could take back some of the things I said to you.''

Heaving an enormous sigh, Cord brought her head to his chest. ''Abbie, we almost destroyed the best chance at happiness any two people ever had. I love you. Why in hell couldn't I say that when you came to me that very first day? We've wasted ten months of our lives.''

Abbie nestled against him, fitting her body to his, reveling in her spiraling emotions. ''They weren't wasted, my love,'' she whispered. ''Not when we're standing here like this, finally together.''

''We're always going to be together, Abbie. From here on in.'' Cord tipped her chin and looked into her misty eyes. ''My own sweet wife. We've got everything going for us, Abbie, good health, each other and a beautiful son.'' His mouth came down slowly to taste hers, but when her lips parted and she kissed him back, he groaned and forgot about everything but the joy of holding her.

He scooped her up and placed her on the bed, following her down to the still partially disheveled blankets. He wriggled out of his clothes between hungry kisses and then was startled to discover that Abbie wore nothing beneath her wraparound. Startled but pleased.

''I was hoping you'd come back soon,'' she breathlessly told him. ''I was going to seduce you if nothing else worked.''

Cord untied the sash at her waist and slid back the two front panels of the pale green garment. He bent to kiss her breasts, each one, then her navel, and finally the sweet curvature of her femininity. His caresses were loving, heated by desire, as always, but containing a tenderness that touched Abbie's soul.

Her eyes had closed to savor more perfectly the sensations he was arousing in her body, but she felt his stare and lifted her lashes. "What is it, Cord?"

"I just thought of something. Sweetheart, I love you so much and our wedding day was a total bust. Will you marry me again?"

"Again?" A slow smile tipped Abbie's lips as the idea sunk in. "Have another ceremony?"

Cord gave a slight nod. "I'm asking, not demanding, honey."

Her smile got broader. "I can tell the difference, my darling, don't worry." Her expression became dreamy. "A real wedding. Oh, Cord, it's an incredible idea. When?"

"You decide." He lowered his head and began nibbling at her neck. "I picked the date of our first wedding, you pick the second." He grinned. "Maybe I'll choose the third."

She laughed lightly, happily. "We'll take turns."

Cord's eyes sobered. "I love you, Abbie. I never gave up on us, you know. And I want you to know something else. There hasn't been another woman since the night we met. I told you there wouldn't be, and there wasn't." He saw something on her face. "Ash is a pesky friend who pops up every so often. We never were intimately involved, Abbie, you have to believe that."

She touched his cheek. "I do, Cord. It bothered me that she called, but you have a right to your friends, male and female. I'm not normally petty about such things. It's just that I was so uncertain and insecure."

"I know, honey, I know." He dipped his head to nuzzle her breasts, whispering, "A man would have to be soft in the head to notice any other woman with you in his bed, sweetheart."

Their conversation fizzled out in the wake of more important considerations.

# Epilogue

Mr. and Mrs. Cord Durants' second wedding took place on the seventeenth of December, which was the first anniversary of the night they met.

Gary and Sherry acted as attendants again, and were aglow from an announcement of their own. "We're going to be married in June."

They were a tightly knit foursome, and Abbie was thrilled that she and Sherry were going to be related.

The wedding and reception were beautiful, and unhurried as this time they had booked the Winston House for the entire afternoon. Friends were delighted to have been invited to share such a romantic occasion, and there was no question that the event was an enormous success.

For Cord and Abbie it was much more than an ordinary renewal of vows. It was the beginning they had missed the first time around, evident to each other in the adoring looks they exchanged during the reception, in the way they had to keep touching, in the whispered and sometimes teasing promises aimed at their wedding night.

They were rarely alone, as everyone had best wishes to pass on to the happy couple. When a break with the mingling crowd finally did occur, Cord speculated on his brother's and Sherry's careers. "What do you think they decided, Abbie?"

"Sherry told me just before the ceremony, Cord. Gary is going to retire from the military."

Cord looked incredulous. "You're kidding."

"He didn't tell you about it?"

"We haven't really talked, honey. He only arrived in town a few hours ago, you know. You mean that they'll be living in Vegas? My God, this is fantastic."

"Sherry said that they talked about it for months. Ran up huge long-distance charges. But in the end they decided that Sherry feels stronger about her career than Gary does."

"He loves the Marine Corps, Abbie."

"Yes, he does." She stood on tiptoe to kiss her husband's cheek. "But he loves Sherry more, my darling. One of them had to concede."

The look that passed between them contained the magic of complete understanding. "I'm sure," Abbie said softly, "that the next time a major decision must be made, Sherry will concede. That's the way it works when two people are truly in love and determined to be together."

Cord put his arm around his wife's waist and drew her closer to his side. "Like us, Abbie."

She smiled. "Precisely, my love."

\*    \*    \*    \*    \*

SILHOUETTE® *Desire*®

MAN OF THE MONTH: 1993

**They're tough, they're sexy...
and they know how to get the
job done....
Caution: They're**

**MEN AT WORK**

Blue collar... white collar... these men are working overtime
to earn your love.

| | |
|---|---|
| July: | Undercover agent Zeke Daniels in Annette Broadrick's ZEKE |
| August: | Aircraft executive Steven Ryker in Diana Palmer's NIGHT OF LOVE |
| September: | Entrepreneur Joshua Cameron in Ann Major's WILD HONEY |
| October: | Cowboy Jake Tallman in Cait London's THE SEDUCTION OF JAKE TALLMAN |
| November: | Rancher Tweed Brown in Lass Small's TWEED |
| December: | Engineer Mac McLachlan in BJ James's ANOTHER TIME, ANOTHER PLACE |

Let these men make a direct deposit into your heart.
MEN AT WORK... only from Silhouette Desire!

MOM93JD

# TAKE A WALK ON THE
# DARK SIDE OF LOVE WITH

October is the shivery season, when chill winds blow and
shadows walk the night. Come along with us into a haunting
world where love and danger go hand in hand, where
passions will thrill you and dangers will chill you. Silhouette's
second annual collection from the dark side of love brings
you three perfectly haunting tales from three of our most
bewitching authors:

## Kathleen Korbel
## Carla Cassidy
## Lori Herter

Haunting a store near you this October.

Only from 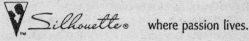 where passion lives.

**by Ann Major**

Take a walk on the wild side with Ann Major's sizzling stories featuring Honey, Midnight...and Innocence!

*IN SEPTEMBER, YOU EXPERIENCED...*

**WILD HONEY** Man of the Month
A clash of wills set the stage for an electrifying romance for J. K. Cameron and Honey Wyatt.

*NOW ENJOY...*

**WILD MIDNIGHT** November 1993
Heat Up Your Winter
A bittersweet reunion turns into a once-in-a-lifetime adventure for Lacy Douglas and Johnny Midnight.

*AND IN FEBRUARY 1994, LOOK FOR...*

**WILD INNOCENCE** Man of the Month
One man's return sets off a startling chain of events for Innocence Lescuer and Raven Wyatt.

Let your wilder side take over with this exciting series—only from Silhouette Desire!

# ▼™ SILHOUETTE® *Desire*™®

## HAS THE WINTER
## WEATHER GOT YOU DOWN?
## IS THE TEMPERATURE
## JUST TOO COLD? THEN

**COMING IN NOVEMBER
ONLY FROM SILHOUETTE DESIRE**

Silhouette Desire's most sensuous writers bring you
six sexy stories—and six stunning heroes—guaranteed
to get your temperature rising.

### Look for

| | |
|---|---|
| #817 | TWEED by Lass Small |
| #818 | NOT JUST ANOTHER PERFECT WIFE by Robin Elliott |
| #819 | WILD MIDNIGHT by Ann Major |
| #820 | KEEGAN'S HUNT by Dixie Browning |
| #821 | THE BEST REVENGE by Barbara Boswell |
| #822 | DANCLER'S WOMAN by Mary Lynn Baxter |

When it comes to sinfully seductive heroes and
provocative love stories...no one does it better than
Silhouette Desire!

SDWH

## Silhouette Books has done it again!

Opening night in October has never been as exciting! Come watch as the curtain rises and romance flourishes when the stars of tomorrow make their debuts today!

*Revel* in Jodi O'Donnell's STILL SWEET ON HIM—
Silhouette Romance #969
...as Callie Farrell's renovation of the family homestead leads her straight into the arms of teenage crush Drew Barnett!

*Tingle* with Carol Devine's BEAUTY AND THE BEASTMASTER—
Silhouette Desire #816
...as legal eagle Amanda Tarkington is carried off by wrestler Bram Masterson!

*Thrill* to Elyn Day's A BED OF ROSES—
Silhouette Special Edition #846
...as Dana Whitaker's body and soul are healed by sexy physical therapist Michael Gordon!

*Believe* when Kylie Brant's McLAIN'S LAW—
Silhouette Intimate Moments #528
...takes you into detective Connor McLain's life as he falls for psychic—and suspect—Michele Easton!

Catch the classics of tomorrow—*premiering* today—
only from **V.** *Silhouette*

## And now for
## something completely different
## from Silhouette....

## SPELLBOUND
### R O M A N C E

Every once in a while, Silhouette brings you a book that is truly unique and innovative, taking you into the world of paranormal happenings. And now these stories will carry our special "Spellbound" flash, letting you know that you're in for a truly exciting reading experience!

In October, look for *McLain's Law* (IM #528) by Kylie Brant

Lieutenant Detective Connor McLain believes only in what he can see—until Michele Easton's haunting visions help him solve a case...and her love opens his heart!

*McLain's Law* is also the Intimate Moments "Premiere" title, introducing you to a debut author, sure to be the star of tomorrow!

Available in October...only from Silhouette Intimate Moments

# SILHOUETTE.... Where Passion Lives

Don't miss these Silhouette favorites by some of our most popular authors!
And now, you can receive a discount by ordering two or more titles!

### *Silhouette Desire®*

| | | | |
|---|---|---|---|
| #05751 | THE MAN WITH THE MIDNIGHT EYES BJ James | $2.89 | ☐ |
| #05763 | THE COWBOY Cait London | $2.89 | ☐ |
| #05774 | TENNESSEE WALTZ Jackie Merritt | $2.89 | ☐ |
| #05779 | THE RANCHER AND THE RUNAWAY BRIDE Joan Johnston | $2.89 | ☐ |

### *Silhouette Intimate Moments®*

| | | | |
|---|---|---|---|
| #07417 | WOLF AND THE ANGEL Kathleen Creighton | $3.29 | ☐ |
| #07480 | DIAMOND WILLOW Kathleen Eagle | $3.39 | ☐ |
| #07486 | MEMORIES OF LAURA Marilyn Pappano | $3.39 | ☐ |
| #07493 | QUINN EISLEY'S WAR Patricia Gardner Evans | $3.39 | ☐ |

### *Silhouette Shadows®*

| | | | |
|---|---|---|---|
| #27003 | STRANGER IN THE MIST Lee Karr | $3.50 | ☐ |
| #27007 | FLASHBACK Terri Herrington | $3.50 | ☐ |
| #27009 | BREAK THE NIGHT Anne Stuart | $3.50 | ☐ |
| #27012 | DARK ENCHANTMENT Jane Toombs | $3.50 | ☐ |

### *Silhouette Special Edition®*

| | | | |
|---|---|---|---|
| #09754 | THERE AND NOW Linda Lael Miller | $3.39 | ☐ |
| #09770 | FATHER: UNKNOWN Andrea Edwards | $3.39 | ☐ |
| #09791 | THE CAT THAT LIVED ON PARK AVENUE Tracy Sinclair | $3.39 | ☐ |
| #09811 | HE'S THE RICH BOY Lisa Jackson | $3.39 | ☐ |

### *Silhouette Romance®*

| | | | |
|---|---|---|---|
| #08893 | LETTERS FROM HOME Toni Collins | $2.69 | ☐ |
| #08915 | NEW YEAR'S BABY Stella Bagwell | $2.69 | ☐ |
| #08927 | THE PURSUIT OF HAPPINESS Anne Peters | $2.69 | ☐ |
| #08952 | INSTANT FATHER Lucy Gordon | $2.75 | ☐ |

|  | AMOUNT | $ _____ |
|---|---|---|
| **DEDUCT:** | **10% DISCOUNT FOR 2+ BOOKS** | $ _____ |
|  | **POSTAGE & HANDLING** | $ _____ |
|  | ($1.00 for one book, 50¢ for each additional) |  |
|  | **APPLICABLE TAXES*** | $ _____ |
|  | **TOTAL PAYABLE** | $ _____ |
|  | (check or money order—please do not send cash) |  |

To order, complete this form and send it, along with a check or money order for the total above, payable to Silhouette Books, to: *In the U.S.*: 3010 Walden Avenue, P.O. Box 9077, Buffalo, NY 14269-9077; *In Canada*: P.O. Box 636, Fort Erie, Ontario, L2A 5X3.

Name: _____

Address: _____ City: _____

State/Prov.: _____ Zip/Postal Code: _____

*New York residents remit applicable sales taxes.
Canadian residents remit applicable GST and provincial taxes.

SBACK-OD